THE OFFICIAL QUI[illegible]ED ON

THE CHRONICLES OF [illegible] MARY'S SERIES

BY JODI TAYLOR

THE THIRSK UNIVERSITY CHALLENGE

COMPILED BY JODIWORLD QUIZMASTER

CHRISTOPHER BOOTE

The Thirsk University Challenge -
The official quiz book based on the
Chronicles of St Mary's series by Jodi Taylor

FIRST EDITION

First published in Great Britain in 2025 by Rushford Editions

Breachfield House, Breachfield, Wareham, Dorset BH20 6DQ

RUSHFORD EDITIONS Published by Rushford Editions

ISBNs:

978-1-0686608-5-6 Quiz book hardback

978-1-0686608-6-3 Quiz book paperback

978-1-0686608-7-0 Quiz book epub

Cover design by: Hazel Cushion

For permissions, inquiries, or more information, contact:

orders@rushford.ltd

INTRO

Why do people like quiz books? Especially quiz books about other books?

There's a grand and long-lived tradition of holding quizzes at conventions, usually connected to the theme of the con (no matter how nebulous the connection) and for some[1] it's their favourite part of the event!

I think it's because we all know and remember different things, and, no matter how empty-headed anyone claims to be, there is that thrill of knowing an answer that has everyone else baffled.

In this book, you will find around 1,600 questions related to the astonishingly varied St Mary's books written by Jodi Taylor, plus some in some way tangentially related to those stories.

The questions are vaguely in order of the events in each book, and very vaguely in chapters by difficulty - so the earlier chapters about one particular book should have answers more easily cudgelled from your brain - but in reality, as everyone knows, there are only two levels of difficulty: Easy (if you know it) and Impossible (if you don't)[2]

Everyone will know the answer to at least some of them, and I hope everyone will be pleasantly surprised by much they remember of Jodi's books - and if not, well, there's always time for another re-reading …

If you want to keep score, award yourself one point for any correct question with a simple answer, and if there are multiple valid answers, one point for each you get right - so for the question "Name the seven Dwarfs in the Disney animated film" you'd get one point each for naming Happy, Sneezy, Dopey, Sleepy, Grumpy, Doc, and Bashful, and nothing for Snorey nor Snow White.

If you think your answer is 'close enough', then give yourself a half point.

I don't hold with negative points for wrong answers, so always take a guess. After all, What Could Possibly Go Wrong?™.

Oh, and there are **SPOILERS EVERYWHERE**!

[1] We know this because there are always some people who say so in their feedback after the convention has finished, and the conventioneers have made their way back to what could laughingly be called 'the real world'. Such people should be kept under a careful eye.

[2] In a competitive quiz, these are, interestingly enough, Easy (someone else's questions) and Impossible (your questions)

FOREWORD FROM JODI TAYLOR

I am delighted to have been asked to provide a foreword for the very first St Mary's quiz book, very grandly – and appropriately – entitled The Thirsk University Challenge Quizbook.

Believe it or not, the idea to compile a quiz book originated from the quiz sessions at Jodiworld this year. And Jodiworld itself was spawned from Discworld a couple of years ago. Which just goes to show that Hazel was right – no need to mention that to her – and going out occasionally and mixing with people in the real world is a good thing after all. Who'd have thought?

I can't imagine the amount of reading and research that must have gone into compiling and checking all the hundreds of questions in this book, although I have to say that I do enjoy getting lost in the research necessary for the Chronicles of St Mary's. Ferreting out obscure facts is great fun. Especially when I tumble across something truly bizarre that I can use for Markham's Fun Facts. The one about all mammals taking twenty-one seconds to empty their bladder has certainly taken on a life of its own. And, in my case, irrevocably altered my bathroom habits. Forever. And those of the entire nation. Listen at any random bathroom door – be very careful how you set about that – and all you can hear is, 'Sixteen Mississippi, seventeen Mississippi, eighteen Mississippi, etc.' And, in my case, there's a bit of slowing down or speeding up in order to land exactly on twenty-one seconds. I should perhaps point out it's the *counting* that alters its speed, rather than the actual … flow. That's something far beyond my simple skills. How did we get on to this subject? Moving on in some haste …

Still vaguely on the subject of research – when I first started writing *Just One Damned Thing After Another*, I did have this weird idea that I, Jodi Taylor, could single-handedly, reinstate History's rightful position in the National Curriculum, although those of my friends who retain a slightly stronger grip on reality have informed me that this is unlikely to happen. I am, however, delighted to say that many people have written to me, saying my books have reawakened their personal interest in History, or telling me how they've gone on to research individual historical events or people because they wanted to know what happened afterwards. And sometimes beforehand, as well. I feel strongly that this should be encouraged. Firkle away, people! Beware rabbit holes, however – one thing can more than lead to another. You can start in 1815 at the Battle of Waterloo – and a couple of keystrokes later you're up to your neck in 5th century BC linothorax. My advice – don't even attempt deep diving without an adequate supply of tea and biscuits and always tell someone where you're going.

Anyway, yet again dragging ourselves back to the subject in hand – the very first St Mary's quiz book – here it is. Massive thanks to Chris Boote who mooted the original idea and compiled the questions, to Karin Mallion from whose giant brain sprang the concept of Jodiworld – and to Hazel Cushion who coordinated everything and, as she always does, brought order out of chaos. The layout is very simple – questions on one page – answers overleaf. This is designed for people like me who continually lose their place when having to turn to the back of the book for the answers. And for those unkind enough to ask – no, I couldn't answer all the questions. So top up your glass/mug/bucket, open the good biscuits and give it a go.

Good luck, everyone!

www.joditaylorbooks.com

CONTENTS

ST MARY'S

St Mary's in an institution (in the sense that all there are more inmates than employees, and are thoroughly institutionalised by being there) where, possibly secretly, most readers of the series would love to work.

They study historical events in contemporary time (and you will be frowned at by the frighteningly vulturine countenance of Dr Bairstow if you call it Time Travel[1]) and always behave in a calm, collected, and, above all, professional manner, with almost never any unexpected set backs.

When you've finished laughing at that, you can try a few of these.

[1] It's Time Travel!

Round One

Questions

1. According to Max, what are the only important things in a pod?
2. What do St Mary's pods always smell of?
3. Why is there no Psychological Monitoring Officer at St Mary's, according to Dr Foster?
4. Where does Leon keep his personal, highly illegal pod?
5. What historical battle re-enactment resulted in the destruction of the clock tower?
6. At St Mary's, if in doubt …?
7. Who was the original director of St Mary's?
8. What relationship are Mrs De Winter and Mrs Partridge?
9. Why is it not necessarily a good thing if the fire alarms in R&D don't go off?
10. What is always a historian's primary survival strategy?
11. What is the best thing about being at St Mary's?
12. What's the worst thing about being at St Mary's?
13. What is the standard pod configuration for long assignments?
14. What is the standard method of St Mary's dealing with a crisis?
15. What's a FOD PLOD?
16. Why is protecting the Archive so vital?
17. What is the unpleasant, largest part of a Historian's job?

Answers

1. Kettle, mugs, biscuit tin, possibly historians
2. Boiled cabbage
3. There were not enough trained professionals in the world to sort out the staff at St Mary's
4. At the back of the paint store
5. The Charge of the Light Brigade
6. Make some tea
7. Dr Bairstow
8. Sisters
9. They probably took the batteries out
10. Running away
11. If you live long enough you get to choose your last jump
12. No one has lived long enough to choose their last jump
13. A three sided square, doors facing inwards
14. Put the kettle on
15. Checking a site for anomalous Foreign Objects and Debris before Jumping home
16. St Mary's can't Jump back to record anything a second time
17. Watching people die

Round Two

Questions

1. What alter ego does Mrs Partridge sometimes go by?
2. Where in London did Matthew live as a child chimney sweep?
3. What was the problem with the genuine Greek Fire that Professor Rapson brought back from ancient Greece?
4. Who has access to the key to Mr Swanson's poison's cabinet?
5. Which member of St Mary's is Vortigern?
6. What are the first names of Professor Rapson and Doctor Dowson?
7. Who are SPOHB?
8. What did Dr Foster's T-shirt say?
9. During the Icarus experiment, who knocked himself out running into a horse's backside?
10. What argument about pay did Max never win with Dr Bairstow?
11. After a St Mary's mission, what defines it being a good day?
12. Who at St Mary's has been nominated for several film & TV awards?
13. What was Max's theory why so many assignments went awry?
14. What is the correct title of St Mary's?
15. Which horse held a long standing grudge against Markham?
16. What are the only rules Mrs Mack abides by?
17. While at St Mary's, which special dessert does Markham have personally served by Janet?

Answers

1. Kleio, the Muse of History
2. Grit Lane
3. No one could put it out
4. Everyone - it's kept in the cabinet door
5. Mrs Mack's cat
6. Andrew and Octavius
7. The Society for the Preservation Of Historical Buildings
8. Does not play well with others
9. Markham
10. Should historians get paid for the actual time they spent on assignment, or the elapsed time they were away from St Mary's?
11. You're alive
12. Mrs Enderby
13. History didn't want them there
14. The Institute of Historical Research at St Mary's Priory
15. Turk
16. The Flour Handling Regulations
17. Spotted Dick

Notes

MAX

Max is the main character in the Chronicles of St Mary's.

After a difficult childhood, she found a passion for history by reading a book, hidden in the back of a wardrobe. With a little push from her teacher Mrs De Winter she decided to attend the University of Thirsk and gained a degree, then a doctorate, in history, specialising in Ancient Civilisations. She travelled and worked abroad for a while before another intervention by Mrs De Winter, which sent her into the welcoming arms of St Mary's Institute of Historical Research. There, she finds that St Mary's uses a much more hands-on approach when it comes to fact-checking historical accuracy...

Now, she skips up and down the timeline to observe major historical events.

If you can call causing chaos and mayhem at any time and place observing, that is

Questions

1. What is Max's full name?
2. What is Max's default state?
3. Why did Max choose her new horn-rimmed glasses?
4. What does Max get the urge to do after drinking eggnog?
5. How bad was Max's sense of direction?
6. What inspired Max's love of History?
7. Which was Max's favourite pod?
8. Why can't Max deal with sympathy?
9. What ubiquitous item didn't Max possess that unnerved others?
10. Why did Max choose History at University?
11. What, as a child, had Max written an 'unsuitable' poem about?
12. Who was the best boss Max ever had?

Answers

1. Dr Madeleine Maxwell
2. In trouble
3. Because they made her look both sexy and intelligent (apparently)
4. Write poetry
5. She once got lost on a staircase
6. A book, "Henry V and the battle of Agincourt"
7. Number Eight
8. She never gets any
9. A mobile phone
10. There was little heavy lifting, and it was out of the wind and rain
11. Cannibalism
12. Bridget Lafferty (until the trying to kill her thing)

Notes

Just One Damned Thing After Another

"So tell me, Dr Maxwell, if the whole of History lay before you... where would you go? What would you like to witness?"

Recruited by the St Mary's Institute of Historical Research, Madeleine Maxwell discovers the Historians there don't just study the past - they revisit it. But one wrong move and History will fight back - to the death. And she soon discovers it's not just History she's fighting...

Round One

Questions

1. Who sent Max to the library instead of expelling her?
2. What colour jumpsuits do IT wear?
3. After brutally sacking Stevens, what nickname did Isabella Barclay acquire?
4. Why did Max choose the pokey attic room in the main building. instead of the large modern room in the Staff block?
5. What happened at the appointed return time from her first jump?
6. Which car did Leon drive Max to Thirsk University in?
7. Where was Max's first working jump?
8. What caused Leon to crash the car into a tree?
9. Who peed on Max?
10. What did Max claim caused Leon to crash the car?
11. What almost happened to Max when she tried to stop a robbery in 1040 London?
12. Where was Max's first Big Job jump?
13. What was Leon's big secret that he told to Max?
14. How did Max and Kal get over the trauma of their hospital ordeal?
15. Who fired Max?
16. What did Max and Dieter find in the Cretaceous?
17. What handmade gift does Leon give Max?
18. What was the only bit of Sussman left on the path?
19. Who stabbed Sussman and left him for the raptors?
20. What did the disc Leon brought to Max show really happened in the Cretaceous?
21. What was Sussman's Big Idea about the Cretaceous project?
22. Where did Leon take Max after showing her the disc?
23. What did Leon hide inside the wooden horse?
24. Who marked Markham's strip poker cards?
25. What did Max find in her filthy jacket pocket that would change the world for ever?
26. Where was the first rescue mission planned for?

Answers

1. Mrs De Winter
2. Black
3. Bitchface
4. It had a bath
5. The computer shut down
6. Dr Bairstow's Bentley
7. The laying of the foundations of Westminster Abbey
8. Max offering him the blow-job of a lifetime
9. Peterson
10. A deer
11. Falling block of masonry
12. A World War 1 Casualty Clearing Centre in France
13. He was from the future
14. They drew it on the sickroom wall
15. Isabella Barclay
16. A dinosaur hunting camp
17. Wooden Horse
18. His foot inside his boot
19. Clive Ronan
20. Sussman attacked her
21. A Day in the Life of a Dinosaur's Waterhole
22. A small island in the Mediterranean about 5,000 years before Max's time
23. His pod remote control
24. Hunter
25. A Cretaceous pinecone
26. The Great Library of Alexandria

Round Two

Questions

1. What penetrating question did Max ask at her interview?
2. How did Sussman get top marks at every Friday exam?
3. What was the point of Outdoor Survival?
4. How did Max deter Whissell from being too in unarmed combat training?
5. What would have been the correct procedure on arriving somewhere not Shrewsbury?
6. Where did Leon let Max hide instead of going on her Outdoor Survival weekend?
7. How did Max deal with Isabella Barclay's fake 'on fire' emergency?
8. What was the name of Clive Ronan's love interest?
9. Where did Max plan to hide while the Outdoor Survival weekend took place?
10. Where did the hospital fire break out?
11. Why was Max's choice of hiding place a mistake?
12. When did Max start to realise the spa break was a setup?
13. Where did the Historians go to get some battlefield medical training?
14. What broke the tension in the pod returning from the hospital fire?
15. Why did Helen say she insisted on separate rooms for the Spa break?
16. What music did Max play over the pod speakers at full volume to signal she had arrived?
17. When crossing over the narrow part of the track, what did Max think happened to her?
18. Who told Leon about the Max's lost baby?
19. How was the pinecone able to be brought out of its own time?
20. What caused the pod to fall down the mountainside?
21. Who opened the dinosaur cages by mistake?
22. What came out of the forest at the same time as Leon and the others?
23. How did Max defuse the riot?
24. Who else was at Mrs De Winter's house when Max brought the men back?
25. Who tried to smash Max's head in with a rock?
26. What did Jenny Fields want to bring back from the past?

Answers

1. "What's Hawking?"
2. He wrote notes on his arms
3. An initiative test to see how well they could get out of it
4. Reached down, grabbed, and twisted
5. Activate emergency extraction
6. In his pod
7. Doused her with ice cold water
8. Annie Bessant
9. Leon's paint store
10. In the blanket store in the linen room
11. It was Inventory weekend, and people would be in and out all day
12. When Peterson's roses matched the ladies' dresses
13. A nearby Army hospital
14. Max threw up on Sussman
15. Kal and Max both snore
16. Lucy in the Sky with Diamonds, from the Beatles' Sergeant Pepper album
17. Raptor attack
18. Isabella Barclay
19. It was about to be destroyed by the fire
20. An earthquake
21. Isabella Barclay
22. A young Tyrannosaurus Rex
23. Challenged Dieter to accompany her on a jump
24. Dr Bairstow
25. Isabella Barclay
26. Dodos

Round Three

Questions

1. What did Max always call Isabella Barclay to her face, knowing how it wound her up?
2. What assignment subject did Mrs De Winter assign a young Madeleine to help her?
3. How did Leon know in advance that something had happened to the crew of pod Number Three?
4. What was odd about the swans on Max's first visit to St Mary's?
5. Why are Historians encouraged to give blood regularly?
6. What did Dr Bairstow tell Max to correct in her personal details form?
7. Who left Max's intake of trainees after breaking his leg?
8. What did Max use code 50A9804B to do? 70.
9. What did Max wear under her authentic 14th Century Shrewsbury costume?
10. Why was Sussman clean and undamaged in the hospital fire?
11. Why did Leon call Max 'Lucy'?
12. At what 'romantic' spot in the hospital did Kal, Sussman, and Max arrange to meet?
13. When did Max realise that the pod failure was deliberate?
14. Why was Max sure she would get the Peterloo jump in Kal's place?
15. What was the best thing Max could say about Sussman?
16. Which raptor species ate Sussman?
17. What personal item had Max hidden in her pack for the Cretaceous assignment?
18. What was Max's Big Idea?
19. Who grabbed Max outside Wardrobe?
20. What was Peterson's Big Idea?
21. What did Isabella Barclay claim Max had done to her?
22. What did Rapson & Dowson fuel the handmade flamethrower with?
23. Who was the first person at the all-staff meeting to understand why the pinecone could leave its own time?
24. How did the rescue jump go wrong?
25. Where did Kleio tell Max there was an anomaly?
26. What did Professor Rapson decide would be the best way to seal the scrolls into jars?

Answers

1. IIzzie
2. The precise nature of Ma'at
3. They were Historians. Something always happened
4. They were blue
5. As an investment for the future
6. She was not 5'7" and never would be
7. Rutherford
8. Restrict access to her pod
9. A sports bra and thermal underwear
10. He'd followed Kal's orders and gone straight to the pod
11. She was the girl with kaleidoscope eyes
12. By the latrines
13. On her third day
14. She was the only female Historian available
15. He's not that bad
16. Deinonychus
17. The photo of her and Leon
18. Make contemporary historic holos to show to the public, without revealing when and where they were filmed
19. Whissell
20. Historical presentations for schools
21. Stolen her life
22. Animal droppings
23. Dieter
24. They arrived one hour late and the library was already on fire
25. Under the fourth step
26. A mixture of pitch and animal dung

Round Four

Questions

1. How did Max make sure the pod wouldn't jump away without her?
2. What summed up the initial relationship between Mrs Partridge and Max?
3. What was the minimum pass mark for all exams?
4. Who was the first to leave from Max's intake?
5. How many days was Max stranded in her first solo jump?
6. Where did Max's first simulation jump to 15th Century Constantinople end up?
7. How did Max first get her card marked during training?
8. Why couldn't Kal go on the Peterloo jump?
9. What was the third thing Max discovered was contagious?
10. What were the first dinosaurs Max and Sussman saw?
11. What Max say was waiting for the men back at Rushford?
12. What had Isabella Barclay said, that made Max realise meant she had deliberately abandoned the men?
13. On which day of the assignment did everything go wrong?
14. Why, as a doctor, was Helen Foster so concerned if Max and Leon had had sex?
15. Who accidentally punched Max in the face in the bar riot?
16. Why did Leon and Max finally get out of the pod shower?
17. What dessert did Max refuse to eat on her Shrewsbury jump?
18. Who ran off to bring back a fork lift truck to smash their way into the crashed pod?
19. Why was everyone to have their heads covered when handling the rescued scrolls?
20. What anomaly did Max see on the ground when running for the pod in the Cretaceous?
21. How did the attackers defeat St Mary's at Site B?
22. Who did Clive Ronan have shot, before he'd even made his demands known?
23. Who cracked, and agreed to open the pods for Clive Ronan?
24. What had Leon and Dieter been doing in Hawking secretly for three days?
25. Why had Leon let Isabella Barclay go?
26. What nickname did Mrs Enderby use for Louise de Kérouaille?

Answers

1. Wedged her basket in the doorway
2. Mrs Partridge made sure to take her pen back
3. 80%
4. Jordan
5. Sixteen
6. Minoan Crete
7. Answering Isabella Barclay's question to Stevens
8. Appendicitis
9. Seeing other people cry
10. Maiasaura
11. Lamb casserole, treacle tart, hot showers, warm beds, and beer
12. She said she saw all four of them dead, but she couldn't have known that Markham wasn't safe in Max's pod
13. Day 74
14. She had a large bet on it with Peterson
15. Dieter
16. They emptied the water tank
17. Stewed apple
18. Polly Perkins
19. Any anomalous hairs with modern hair products would cast doubt upon their authenticity
20. A piece of dark green metal with the letters "RD T" on it
21. They snuck round behind them
22. Young Jamie Cameron
23. Leon
24. Turning TB2 into a giant EMP triggered bomb
25. In the hope she would lead them to Clive Ronan
26. The French Strumpet

Notes

A Symphony of Echoes

Dispatched to Victorian London to seek out Jack the Ripper, things go badly wrong when he finds the St Mary's Historians first. Stalked through the fog-shrouded streets of Whitechapel, Max is soon running for her life. Again.

And that's just the start. Max finds herself in a race against time when an old enemy is intent on destroying St Mary's. An enemy willing, if necessary, to destroy History itself.

From the Hanging Gardens to the murder of Thomas à Becket, via an unscheduled dodo rescue mission, join the Historians of St Mary's as they hurtle around History on more hilarious, hair-raising escapades

Round One

Questions

1. Where was Kal's last jump as a Historian?
2. How did Max and Kal realise something was in the pod with them?
3. Who became Max's assistant?
4. Who was the new head of IT?
5. What did Max make as part of her rehab?
6. Where did Max and Petersen take future St Mary's for their first real assignment since the attack?
7. Who shot Isabella Barclay?
8. Who was the nasty piece of work running the Rehab centre where Max and Leon were sent?
9. Who did Max say was the most important department?
10. What anomaly was revealed in the newly discovered Shakespeare play?
11. What seven-stop treat was arranged to let new recruits get familiar with Pod travel?
12. What did Leon say that shattered Max to the core?
13. What did Max's St Mary's Dr Bairstow hide under the fourth step?
14. How did Max always refer to Mary, Queen of Scots?
15. Who did Max appoint as the new Director of future St Mary's?
16. Who did Max walk into, in the dark and the rain in Edinburgh?
17. Where did Dr Bairstow send Max and Leon to recuperate?
18. What was Max's reward for saving History?
19. Which Pathfinders' assignment did Peterson suggest to Max to take her mind off things?
20. What two things did Sands have an inexhaustible supply of?
21. Who locked Mary Queen of Scots in a room with the rapist Bothwell?
22. What project were Sands and Professor Rapson working on?

Answers

1. Whitechapel, 1888
2. It moved Max's muff
3. David Sands
4. Polly Perkins
5. A ten-foot long scarlet snake
6. The murder of Thomas à Becket, Canterbury Cathedral, 1170
7. Max
8. Alexander Knox
9. The Kitchen crew
10. Mary Queen of Scots did not marry Bothwell
11. Seven wonders of the world
12. "I don't think so, Dr Maxwell, do you?"
13. The Shakespearean sonnets
14. The Tartan Trollop
15. Pinkie
16. A young Clive Ronan
17. The Red House (the Redhouse Centre)
18. Troy
19. The Hanging Gardens of Nineveh, 680BC
20. Chocolate and Knock-knock jokes
21. Max
22. Fitting blades to his wheelchair

Round Two

Questions

1. Who else saw the Ripper's decapitated head move?
2. In which pub did they look for Mary Kelly?
3. Who went missing after disposing of the last of the Ripper?
4. What story did Tim tell the future St Mary's about Max to make them trust her?
5. What did Clive Ronan want from St Mary's?
6. Which site was the first jump after the attack?
7. Who was in future St Mary's with Clive Ronan?
8. What was fishy about Alexander Knox's past?
9. Why did the third of the 'Wonders' jumps, to the Hanging Gardens of Babylon, not go well?
10. Where did Max go to investigate Knox?
11. Where did Max leave Leon's car?
12. Who was deliberately changing History in Mary, Queen of Scot's time?
13. What went wrong with the initial jump to Nineveh?
14. What happened to Mr Hopwood at Nineveh?
15. Why did St Mary's need to rent a big house in the Canongate area of Edinburgh?
16. For whom did Sennacherib build Nineveh's beautiful royal palace and gardens?
17. What time-honoured method did St Mary's use to get themselves noticed in Edinburgh?
18. Why did Dr Foster not try everything to save David Sand's life?
19. What trade did the St Mary's crew adopt to get an audience with Queen Mary?
20. Who had hidden the history book in child Madeleine's wardrobe?
21. How did Max lure Queen Mary into Bothwell's room?
22. What did Mrs Partridge pack for a day of dodo wrangling?

Answers

1. Major Guthrie
2. The Ten Bells, Spitalfields
3. Leon
4. The Cretaceous rescue and fighting a Tyrannosaurus Rex
5. The pods
6. The Pyramids at Giza
7. Isabella Barclay
8. He didn't appear to have one
9. They couldn't find them
10. Director Pinkerton's St Mary's
11. In the lake at St Mary's
12. Clive Ronan
13. They arrived a year early
14. Stung by a scorpion
15. The had to give the impression of wealthy, high-class, traders
16. His wife
17. Spend, spend, spend!
18. He had signed a 'Do Not Resuscitate' order months before
19. Cloth merchants
20. Leon
21. She told her Leon was there waiting to play chess with her
22. Afternoon Tea

Round Three

Questions

1. What colour code did Max call when returning from Victorian London with Kalinda Black?
2. How many future St Mary's personnel had Clive Ronan killed?
3. What part of the Ripper had Helen saved in case of infection?
4. When did Max realise the perks of being Director?
5. Where had Pinkie hidden the data cube?
6. What was the first sign the Red House wasn't on the NHS?
7. Why had Leon been so brutal to Max at the Red House?
8. What was Max sure was the sign of a diseased mind?
9. Who was Alexander Knox really?
10. What was causing Leon's vivid dreams?
11. Who was secretly one of Clive Ronan's men all along?
12. Why didn't Director Knox give Clive Ronan the coordinates of the backup site when he gave him everything else?
13. What message did Peterson write on the wall to tell future St Mary's when they were?
14. What was James Bothwell's preferred 'type'?
15. What did Leon offer as a personal gift when the attempted arrival of Bothwell soured the Queen's mood?
16. Why didn't History eliminate Clive Ronan when he tampered with it?
17. Who did Max assign to find out where reality and the Shakespearean Mary Queen of Scots play diverged?
18. Where was Mrs De Winter while Max and Mrs Partridge were in Mauritius?
19. Who did Max 'describe as sex on legs'?
20. What was the only noticeable change after Dr Bairstow's training seminar on 'Caring Management'?
21. Why was Max relived to see the bleeding wound on Major Guthrie's forehead?
22. What interrupted Max and Leon's reconciliation after Nineveh?

Answers

1. Code Blue
2. Thirteen
3. A smear of its blood
4. When she got chocolate digestives with her tea
5. In a fire bucket in her office
6. They had carpets
7. Knox had said it was the only 'treatment' that would work
8. Matching curtains and bedcovers
9. Pinkie's missing director
10. Bleed-through
11. Evan
12. Mrs Partridge had swapped the coordinates in the safe for something deadly
13. 681BC
14. Female, with a pulse
15. A jade chess set
16. He was still young, it would have created a paradox
17. Van Owen and Schiller
18. Bolivia
19. James, Earl of Bothwell
20. He had some armchairs installed in his office
21. Dead people don't bleed
22. The fire alarm went off when Markham set fire to the curtains in Sick Bay

Round Four

Questions

1. What had SPOHB morphed into?
2. How many whacks with the axe did it take to behead the Ripper?
3. Who was the future St Mary's kitchen supremo?
4. Who offered Max and Kal a drink in a Whitechapel pub?
5. Who does Peterson always go as for fancy dress parties?
6. What did Kal demand after the final destruction of the Ripper?
7. Who did Max & Peterson see being murdered in Nineveh?
8. What was the name of Leon's nurse?
9. What excuse did Max give to leave the room but keep Bothwell there?
10. How many dodos did Max and Mrs Partridge rescue?
11. How did Max recognise the house from Leon's dreams?
12. Why was Thomas Becket wearing green robes at the time of his murder?
13. Who did Max send to 16th Century Istanbul and Bursa to buy cloths and fabrics to impress the Queen?
14. Who was Clive Ronan's accomplice, Michel de Castelnau?
15. Why is it a bad idea to throw hot ashes over a midden?
16. What did Max wear as Caretaker Director of future St Mary's?
17. What were the Queen's four main ladies in waiting known as?
18. How did Pinkie's Mrs Partridge differ from Max's?
19. Why was the Tech Team's attempts at finding dodo nests fruitless?
20. What was kept in Max's desk draw in an envelope labelled "STD Clinic - t est results"?
21. Who was the doctor assigned to Max and Leon at the Red House?
22. According to Leon, what was the accepted History Department methodology?

Answers

1. SPERM
2. Eleven
3. Christine
4. George Carter
5. Robin Hood
6. Pancakes
7. King Sennacherib
8. Katie Carr
9. To get some wine for them
10. Seventeen
11. Two eagles over the door, one with a broken wing
12. The end of the Catholic year reverted to Ordinary Time after Christmas, and the Ordinary robes are green
13. Mrs Enderby
14. The French Ambassador
15. Methane from the 'human waste'
16. A Historian-blue uniform
17. The Four Marys
18. She had ash-blonde hair
19. They looked in the trees. Dodos were flightless
20. Her chequebook
21. Dr Joanna Trent
22. Bumble around in the dark until they find something they didn't know they were looking for

Notes

WHEN A CHILD IS BORN

It's Christmas Day 1066 and a team from St Mary's is going to Westminster Abbey. Or so they think...

Because History seems to have different plans for them and when Max finds herself delivering a child in a peasant's hut, she can't help wondering what History is up to.

Questions

1. What were the Historians supposed to witness?
2. What did Markham spot in the snow?
3. What should they have done?
4. What did Markham smell?
5. Who was in the hut?
6. What was the woodcutter's name?
7. What effect did Max's whacking of his bottom have on the newborn baby?
8. What did the woodcutter name his new son?
9. Why did Max fail to find the Hanging Gardens of Babylon?
10. Who cooked for everyone?
11. Who was the historically important one in the hut?
12. Which vitally important historical figure would never have been born if Max hadn't interfered?

Answers

1. The coronation of William I
2. Blood
3. Left the woodcutter to die in the snow
4. Woodsmoke
5. A pregnant woman
6. Aelfric
7. He sneezed
8. Harald
9. The were actually in Nineveh
10. Markham
11. Little Aline
12. Simon de Montfort

Notes

A SECOND CHANCE

Max could have been a bomb-disposal expert, or a volunteer for the Mars mission, or a firefighter, something safe and sensible. But, no, she had to be an Historian.

It began well. A successful assignment to 17th century Cambridge to meet Isaac Newton. So far so good.

But then came the long-awaited jump to the Trojan War that changed everything. And for Max, nothing will ever be the same again.

With the bloody Battle of Agincourt playing out around her, Max risks everything on one last desperate gamble to save a life and learns the true meaning of a second chance.

Round One

Questions

1. What happened to the entire history department while Max was away?
2. What did Max want to hire from Mrs Mack?
3. Who was Professor Penrose going to visit as a retirement present from Dr Bairstow?
4. What was Max's preferred quality in a husband?
5. What item caused students to think Max & the Professor were thieves?
6. What did Max's use of a stun gun lead to accusations of?
7. Where in Cambridge did Max take Professor Penrose?
8. Where did Max and Professor Penrose end up when trying to Jump home?
9. Why was everything sticky in the stacks?
10. Who was the Trojan warrior with the red horsehair helmet crest?
11. When the Greeks left Troy, where was the Wooden Horse?
12. Who rescued Max from the Greeks?
13. What caused the mass sickness in Troy?
14. Why couldn't St Mary's get to the upper city of Troy?
15. Who came off worse at Troy in a confrontation with a small flock of geese?
16. Where was Max taken?
17. What happened historically at the Gates of Grief?
18. What was hit by the final bullet in Ronan's pod?
19. Who faked the message from Mr Strong to get Max to the stables?
20. Who was knocking on the damaged pod's door?
21. How did Max die?
22. Who knocked Peterson unconscious at Agincourt?

Answers

1. Dyed themselves blue
2. The entire stock of St Mary's butter
3. Isaac Newton
4. Absence
5. Mirror
6. Witchcraft
7. Trinity College
8. Nowhere, or the birth of Universe
9. It was covered in honey
10. Hector
11. There wasn't one
12. Major Guthrie
13. Eating the infected horses
14. Guards turned every one away
15. Markham
16. The Cretaceous
17. Humankind's only successful migration out of Africa
18. The console
19. Clive Ronan
20. Leon
21. Stabbed by a French soldier
22. Max

Round Two

Questions

1. Why was Leon so certain living with Max would never be boring?
2. What extensive risk assessment had Peterson carried out before the Monolith Experiment?
3. From which author did Max find that butter removes blue dye?
4. What was the cause of the toxic honey?
5. How long did Dr Bairstow say the hallucinogens in the honey would last?
6. How many people did Max say a butchered cow could feed?
7. What was Professor Penrose's suggestion for getting the pod to work again?
8. Who was missing when Max and Major Guthrie got back to the pod?
9. Why did Leon and Major Guthrie let Max out of the pod first at Troy?
10. Who did Max refuse to allow into the pod?
11. Who first realised what was about to happen at Troy?
12. Who called Max with a very bad signal?
13. What brought down the walls of Troy?
14. Who wanted to observe the cheese rolling?
15. Where did Max tell the others to pick her up as Troy fell?
16. What was supposed to be Leon's next assignment after the Cretaceous Jump?
17. What gift did Person give to the survivors of the crossing of the Gates of Grief?
18. What did the peasant slash Peterson's arm with at Agincourt?
19. How did Leon rescue Helios from Troy?
20. Who was waiting for Max in Leon's flat?
21. Who's flat did Max find herself in after her stabbing?
22. What did Leon say first to Max when she came to his workshop?

Answers

1. He'd seen her cook
2. He'd asked Professor Rapson if he thought it would all be OK
3. PG Wodehouse (in Thank you, Jeeves)
4. Bees collecting pollen from rhododendrons
5. 12 hours
6. 1000
7. To open the door and let a tiny bit of 'something' get out and collide with 'nothing'
8. Leon
9. To avoid being trampled into the dirt by her rushing out
10. Helios
11. Major Guthrie
12. Leon
13. An earthquake
14. Everyone
15. On the beach
16. To put the history book in child Madeleine's wardrobe
17. Chocolate
18. A rusty scythe
19. He used his remote to call up his own pod
20. Mrs Partridge
21. Leon's
22. "Isabella?"

Round Three

Questions

1. What did Professor Penrose make Max promise?
2. Who were Max and Kal disappointed never to see in the first stint at Troy?
3. What was St Mary's Plan B never-failing method of communication?
4. Who fell and got her foot wedged in the rubble at Troy?
5. What was Markham and Roberts' punishment for stealing a chicken dedicated to the temple??
6. What did Dr Bairstow find so unnerving about Max on her return from Troy?
7. Who fired the arrow that killed Achilles?
8. With what subject did Max think Major Guthrie had an unhealthy obsession?
9. What happened after the walls of Troy fell?
10. On the Troy assignment, why was Max relegated to unskilled labour when dividing camp duties?
11. How had Paris been killed by the Greeks?
12. What gift did the survivors of the Gates of Grief leave for Max?
13. Who never went to Troy despite the stories and myths?
14. What did Leon ask Max to do after he brought her back from the Cretaceous?
15. How did Leon die?
16. What did Max use to fight off a Deinonychus?
17. What is the most important rule about watching cheese rolling?
18. Why did Max recognise the green cloak Mrs Enderby supplied for the Agincourt Jump?
19. What did Henry V do the night before Agincourt?
20. On which day was the Battle of Agincourt fought?
21. Why was Leon so horrified to see Max?
22. After she'd been stabbed in the chest at Agincourt, on to what did Max fall?

Answers

1. If things didn't work out with Leon, to give him first refusal
2. Helen of Troy
3. Saying nothing and looking stupid
4. Prentiss
5. One month latrine duty
6. Her docility
7. Paris
8. Latrines
9. The Greeks came back
10. No one sane would eat her cooking, and she had nearly amputated her own foot last time she used an axe
11. Hung on the Dardanian Gate and used as a target for the archers
12. A shell necklace
13. Helen
14. To come away with him
15. Massive heart attack
16. (Empty) fire extinguisher
17. Watch the cheese, not the runners, until the cheese has passed you
18. It was the one she wore on her very first Jump
19. Walked from campfire to campfire, talking to every one of his soldiers
20. St Crispin's day (25th October 1415)
21. In his world, she had died
22. A hard, hairy carpet

Round Four

Questions

1. As part of the prep for the Troy Jump, how did Helen Foster put everyone off their lunch?
2. Why was Leon so amazed that Max and Professor Penrose had managed to set fire to the pod?
3. In Max's experience throughout history, when is the only time women walked in front of men?
4. According to Professor Penrose, who did Joan of Arc misquote?
5. Who spoke to Max in English in Athena's temple?
6. Who did one of the evil-eyed goats at the Troy site remind Max of?
7. What was Dr Bairstow's advice to Max to get over the traumas of Troy?
8. Who killed Kassandra and Agamemnon?
9. What was Roberts and Markham's suggestion for the Jump assignments?
10. What was Roberts' backup non-beer related suggestion for a Jump?
11. How did Max get Dr Bairstow to talk about Leon?
12. What is the Maxwell Way?
13. Where did Max wake up after the cheese rolling Jump?
14. Who sounded the alarm to alert Henry that the French prisoners were treacherously taking up arms?
15. What was the thing early Phoenician traders most likely left behind in Britain?
16. What did Max demand of Mrs Partridge before agreeing to anything?
17. Why did Max tell Leon he had to take the assignment from Dr Bairstow even though he thought it beneath him?
18. What did Mrs Partridge say Max was to do?
19. Why did Max and Peterson need to get back to the English baggage train at Agincourt?
20. What favour did Joe Nelson ask of Max?
21. With what did Max attack Leon when he called her 'Isabella'?
22. What was Dr Bairstow's urgent message on the answering machine?

Answers

1. An illustrated presentation of Bronze Age diseases and treatment
2. They had been to Cambridge, the wettest city in the Fens, the wettest part of England
3. When there were minefields
4. Terry Pratchett
5. Kassandra
6. Rosie Lee
7. Paint
8. Agamemnon's wife Clytemnestra
9. Three important events in the history of beer
10. The dancing mania of Aix la Chappelle, 1374
11. Asked him about their epic fight in a Parisian street
12. When you've screwed up, jump in with both feet and make things worse
13. Sick Bay. Again
14. Peterson
15. A generation of half Briton, half Phoenician children
16. To say goodbye to Peterson
17. Because he was special
18. Her best
19. To find out why Henry ordered the French prisoners killed
20. To see Leon's memorial stone in the St Mary's graveyard
21. Blue plastic dustpan
22. "Get out. They're here. Run"

Notes

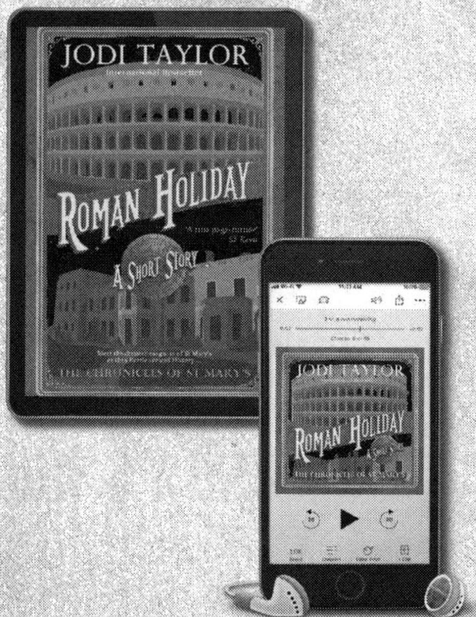

Roman Holiday

Question - What sort of idiot installs his mistress in his wife's house? Especially when that mistress is Cleopatra VII Thea Philopator, Queen of Egypt and the most notorious woman of her time?

Answer - Julius Caesar – poised to become King of Rome.

At this potentially sensitive point in his political manoeuvrings, who are the last people he'd want crashing through the door, observing, recording, documenting, starting a stampede ...?

Questions

1. Who was wrapped in a carpet to be unrolled for Dr Bairstow?
2. What were Markham's bosoms made from?
3. Why did it take three people to hire a carrying chair for Max?
4. Who admitted the Historians into Caesar's house?
5. Which animals were on the house's frescos?
6. What was Max's first impression of Cleopatra?
7. For what did Cleopatra wait before sitting in her throne?
8. Who presented Max and Peterson to Cleopatra?
9. When Caesar arrived, what delicacy was served?
10. Who spotted the asps in the bowl?
11. What did Max fake to gain a reason to leave?
12. Who probably put the snakes in the bowl?
13. When did the legionaries try to stop the Historians?
14. What methods did the Romans try to open the pod?
15. What device did Peterson unveil in an attempt to make the crowds and soldiers leave?
16. Who did Markham suggest they sell the device to?
17. What caused the disaster upon returning to Hawking?

Answers

1. Markham
2. Half-lemons
3. They were all men
4. His wife's Greek secretary
5. Lions
6. Ugly
7. Everyone to bow their heads
8. Calpurnia
9. Figs in honey
10. Markham
11. Heart attack
12. Calpurnia
13. Once they dismissed their carrying chair nowhere near the Street of Six Vines
14. Kicking it, a battering ram, setting fire to it
15. The Sonic Scream
16. Asterix the Gaul
17. The Sonic Scream was still on

Notes

A Trail Through Time

From a 17th-century Frost Fair to Ancient Egypt; from Pompeii to 8th-century Scandinavia; Max and Leon are pursued up and down the timeline, playing a dangerous game of hide-and-seek, until finally they're forced to take refuge at St Mary's where a new danger awaits them.

Max's happily ever after is going to have to wait a while…

Round One

Questions

1. How long did Max and Leon have in peace and safety together?
2. Why was 17th Century London so cold?
3. What did the emergency extraction Jump them to?
4. Who had grassed up Max and Leon to the Time Police?
5. What weapons did the Time Police use when trying to apprehend Max?
6. How were the Time Police tracking Max & Leon?
7. Where did Max and Leon Jump to from the Frost Fair?
8. What was Skaxos?
9. What were the only things Max grabbed when told to get anything valuable?
10. Why couldn't Leon remove the tag from Max's arm?
11. How did Leon's Max die?
12. What was Max's brilliant idea to escape the Time Police?
13. What was the very bad bit of Max's plan to escape the Time Police?
14. Who first came to Sick Bay to interrogate Max?
15. Who did the Time Police arrest in TB2?
16. Which Time Police Officer tried to interrogate Max?
17. What was Helios' new identity in the 'now'?
18. Who was the first person Max recognised in the Great Hall?
19. What did Mrs Mack and the civilian staff throw down at the Time Police?
20. What was the purpose of the hearing at St Mary's?
21. Who lost his foot in the Battle of St Mary's?
22. What did Peterson catch on a trip to see Geoffrey Chaucer?

Answers

1. Less than one day
2. Britain was in the middle of a six hundred year mini-Ice Age
3. A Frost Fair
4. Isabella Barclay
5. Sonics
6. Her tag was still in her arm
7. The Central Asian steppes
8. Leon's secret island
9. Her Trojan Horse, her book on Agincourt, the photo of her and Leon, and her red snake
10. He operated on the wrong arm
11. Carbon monoxide poisoning
12. For Leon to leave her somewhere, and go back to St Mary's to recalibrate and restock the pod
13. Leon would have to surgically remove her tag
14. Isabella Barclay
15. Leon
16. Colonel Albay
17. Joe Nelson, from the pub
18. David Sands
19. Condoms filled with flour
20. To establish Max's identity
21. David Sands
22. The pox - no, the Black Death

Round Two

Questions

1. Where did Max suggest as somewhere quiet, sunny, and warm to Jump to so they could recharge the pod's batteries?
2. Who was Max hoping to see in Egypt?
3. What effect did the Time Police sonics have on the River Nile?
4. How did Max and Leon manage to escape from the ceremony?
5. In the Escape of Queen Mathilda in the Snow experiment, who was left dangling from a bedsheet?
6. Who was riding a horse backwards as part of the Parthian experiment?
7. Why did Markham and Roberts end up freezing their privy members in the snow?
8. Why was the DNA test not usable as evidence?
9. What almost made Max talk?
10. Why couldn't the Time Police use their Truth Cuff on Max's correct arm?
11. How did Helen Foster save Max from interrogation?
12. Where did the monk take Max and Peterson in medieval London?
13. Who snuck into Sick Bay in the dead of night to see Max?
14. How did Peterson contract the Plague?
15. Who did Max see up in the gallery during the Time Police attack?
16. What gift did Leon bring Max in Sick Bay?
17. What did Mrs Partridge throw into the flour-filled Great Hall?
18. What did Max say to bring next time?
19. How did Colonel Albay try to kill Max?
20. What had Isabella Barclay done in Max's room?
21. Who lead the charge by the household staff of St Mary's to repel the Time Police?
22. Who was enjoying the special care so much they pretended they were still blind?

Answers

1. Eighteenth Dynasty Ancient Egypt
2. Pharaoh Akhenaten the Heretic
3. It enraged all the crocodiles
4. By helping a woman with her children
5. Clerk
6. Markham
7. For historical authenticity they hadn't worn any underwear
8. The samples were very close but not identical
9. Two giant bars of chocolate
10. It was still too swollen after Leon's botched attempts to remove Max's tag
11. Told the Time Police she had so many drugs inside her, any method of interrogation would be fruitless
12. St Thomas Hospital
13. Leon
14. Fleas in the mattress
15. Isabella Barclay
16. Bear 2.0
17. A fizzer
18. Jaffa Cakes
19. Suffocation
20. Destroyed and dismembered Bear 2.0
21. Theresa Mack and Mavis Enderby
22. Markham

Round Three

Questions

1. Who helped Max pull Leon out of the Great Drain?
2. What were the only clothes Max had with her when she fled Leon's flat?
3. What unexpected problem had Leon encountered at St Mary's?
4. How was Ellis trapped in Pompeii?
5. What was Professor Rapson's diversion?
6. Who did Roberts and Markham take upstairs and couldn't get down again?
7. Who invited Max to tea?
8. What music did R&D play as they pushed the fireboat towards the jetty?
9. Who was the first person to say they believed Max when she said she was Dr Maxwell?
10. What turned out to be a bigger danger than the fireboat?
11. Why was Max found 'not guilty' of smuggling Helios to the present?
12. How did Max treat Peterson?
13. What did Dr Bairstow offer Max?
14. What information had been brought to Dr Bairstow's attention?
15. Why wasn't Peterson allowed into the hospital?
16. What did Mrs Mack interrupt Dr Bairstow's meeting to demand everyone hand over?
17. What weapons of mass destruction had Professor Rapson and Dr Dowson prepared?
18. What role did Dr Bairstow offer Max if she stayed at St Mary's?
19. Who grabbed Max's ankle to stop her joining the charge?
20. What bribe was Max also offered?
21. Who refused to sign the Charter disbanding the Time Police?
22. Who was the new Acting Director of St Mary's?

Answers

1. Two slaves
2. Yellow and white spotted pyjamas, slippers, and a dressing gown
3. The Time Police were already there, looking for Helios
4. Trapped beneath an overturned food stall and brazier
5. Replicating the fireboats at Tyre
6. Turk, the horse
7. Dr Dowson
8. Mars, the Bringer of War
9. Professor Rapson
10. The swans
11. She wasn't the 'real' Max in this timeline
12. Sterilised his knife in a fire and lanced the swelling
13. An assignment to 14th Century London with Peterson
14. The date of the Time Police attack on his St Mary's
15. He was unconscious, so could not make Confession
16. Condoms
17. A home-made flamethrower, caltrops, a crossbow, some Molotov cocktails, and a World War 1 Vickers gun
18. Chief Operations Officer
19. Mrs Partridge
20. A Jump, anywhere, anywhen, to see anything, with any team she liked
21. Pinkie (and then Max)
22. Leon

Round Four

Questions

1. Why couldn't Ellis call the other Time Police for help in Pompeii?
2. Who was the beautiful wife of Akhenaten?
3. How was Max able to convince Madame President to shut down the hearing?
4. Where in Pompeii did the pod Jump to?
5. Who was missing from St Mary's?
6. Why had Leon been two hours late picking up Max at Pompeii?
7. Who came to Max in her awful little room?
8. What was the punchline of Max's joke?
9. Which large ginger hairy usually immobile member of the St Mary's Kitchen Crew made his debut in this book?
10. When was Helios returned to Troy??
11. What life-saving offer did Mrs Mack make to Max?
12. Who was serving as Colonel Albay's PA during his sojourn at St Mary's?
13. What happened to Peterson after his blazing row with Max in London?
14. Who left Max a copy of the local paper with the details of a terrible road accident?
15. Which pub was the favoured departure point for pilgrims in medieval London?
16. What was the medieval monk's name?
17. What was on the hidden data stick?
18. What names did Max give for herself and Peterson at the hospital?
19. How was the historic Treaty of St Mary's recorded?
20. What did Max say that convinced Peterson she wasn't his Maxwell?
21. Who had murdered the other Maxwell?
22. How did Leon and Max make the decision on whether to leave St Mary's or stay?

Answers

1. The eruption blocked their equipment signals
2. Nefertiti
3. By telling the absolute truth
4. The North-east, next to the amphitheatre
5. Mrs Partridge
6. The pod safety protocols wouldn't let him Jump to the right time and place
7. Kleio, the Muse of History
8. We're having a new kitchen
9. Vortigern
10. Troy, one year after the fall
11. Cocoa
12. Rosie Lee
13. He was knocked on the head in an alley
14. David Sands
15. The Tabard
16. Brother Anselm
17. The location of the remote site
18. Philippa and Thomas of Rushford
19. In red felt-tip pen on a page torn from a notebook
20. She talked about the sensible option
21. Isabella Barclay
22. They flipped a coin

Notes

CHRISTMAS PRESENT

It's Christmas Eve at St Mary's, and all through the house nothing is stirring...

Except for Max, Peterson and Markham, sneaking out at midnight for an assignment that is very definitely off the books.

It's ten years ago tonight that Senior Historians Bashford and Grey went missing in 12th century Jerusalem. So how did they end up in AD60 Roman Colchester?

Max has a theory. Peterson has a plan. Markham has bacon sandwiches. Colchester has Boudica and her bloodthirsty Iceni hordes.

And then there's the giant pig ... the enraged, giant pig...

Questions

1. Where did Mrs Partridge take Max in the middle of the night?
2. Where were Bashford and Grey going to jump to?
3. Which pod did Clive Ronan steal?
4. Who was the only person Max could trust to look after Major Guthrie?
5. Why was Markham prowling the corridors at midnight?
6. What did Max realise had happened to Bashford and Grey?
7. Where had the pod jumped to after Jerusalem?
8. What did Markham say Hunter had told him to bring to their date?
9. What was the sole concession to historical authenticity the team agreed to?
10. What will you invariably find in any quiet back alley anywhen in history?
11. Near to which large building did the team arrive?
12. Which two British tribes had surrounded the town?
13. Who did Markham assign to lookout on the pod roof?
14. Who made up the bulk of the town's defenders?
15. What was Bashford's reaction on seeing Max?
16. What was in the shed that Max set alight?
17. Who waved and shouted "Cooee!" to Boudica?
18. Which goddess did Max tell Boudica she was a messenger from?
19. What defined Bashford as a natural Historian?
20. What gift did Max bring for Mrs Partridge?

Answers

1. Hawking, ten years previously
2. 12th century Jerusalem
3. Number Four
4. Leon
5. Waiting for Hunter to come off shift
6. Ronan had Jumped them to an unknown destination and abandoned them
7. Roman Colchester, 60 AD
8. A tin of Swarfega and a wetsuit
9. Grey woollen cloaks
10. A pod and a couple of bickering Historians. (Wave to them)
11. The Temple of Claudius
12. Iceni and Trinovantes
13. Max
14. Roman legion veterans
15. He tried to punch her
16. A very angry pig and her farrow
17. Bashford
18. Andred the war goddess
19. Completely oblivious of the danger he was in
20. A drawing of the Muses

Notes

No Time Like The Past

The St Mary's Institute of Historical Research has finally recovered from its wounds and it's business as usual for those rascals in the History Department.

From being trapped in the Great Fire of London to an unfortunately timed comfort break at Thermopylae which leaves the fate of the western world hanging in the balance, Max must struggle to get History back on track.

But first, they must get through the St Mary's Fete - which is sure to end badly for everyone.

Only one thing is certain, life at St Mary's is never dull!

Round One

Questions

1. What promotion had Markham received?
2. What was the problem with the permanent hair lacquer invented by R&D?
3. How did Max and Peterson generally amuse themselves during all-staff briefings?
4. What had Dr Bairstow agreed to, after being ambushed by Thirsk?
5. In which conflict did the Lacey brothers end up on opposing sides?
6. What had Max been ambushed by Dr Bairstow to agree to?
7. Who saw the ghost falling past the window?
8. Who burst into tears at the sight of a broken Markham?
9. Where was chosen as a safe, sedate, peaceful Jump?
10. Who was the falling ghost?
11. Where did the recovery team want to go in 1666 to rescue some documents?
12. Which family owned the past St Mary's?
13. Who never returned from the document recovery assignment?
14. What did they find buried in the grounds of St Mary's instead of the priceless documents?
15. Who was the first to end up in the lake during the boat race?
16. What bombshell did Isabella Barclay drop on Max?
17. What was one reason was Max bullied at school?
18. Which artist's works did the recovery team attempt to save when Jumping back to the 1497 Bonfire of the Vanities?
19. Who was Max's new PA?
20. What was Peterson's wedding gift to Max?
21. Who crashed Dr Bairstow's Bentley this time?
22. Who brought a backup car after Max crashed into a tree?

Answers

1. Second-in-charge of the Security Section
2. It was incredibly flammable
3. Sat at the back and played Battleships
4. A boat race between Thirsk and St Mary's on the lake during the Open Day
5. The English Civil War
6. Organising the Open Day and boat race
7. Markham
8. Hunter
9. The Great Exhibition, London, 1851
10. Markham
11. St Paul's Cathedral
12. Lacey
13. Mary Schiller
14. Mary Schiller's body
15. Markham
16. That they were half-sisters
17. Her red hair
18. Botticelli
19. The lovely Mrs Shaw
20. Thermopylae
21. Max
22. Major Guthrie

Round Two

Questions

1. How was Max occupied when the Open Day was mentioned at the briefing?
2. How did Max incapacitate one of Rupert's men?
3. Where did Lady Lacey intend to hide with her boys?
4. Who knocked out Lord Lacey so his wife & her son could escape?
5. Where did the team spend the night in during their jump to St Mary's?
6. What was Max's signal to David Sands to take action?
7. Who came out of their room behind the Historians?
8. Where would the items rescued from St Paul's be concealed?
9. How did Markham survive the fall from the roof?
10. Which favourite of Max's accompanied the bigwigs from Thirsk?
11. Which item was the subject of much double-entendre by the lady Historians?
12. What did Max destroy in her murderous rage?
13. What awkward assessment task did Max have to do?
14. Who came up behind Max and gave her some astonishingly good advice?
15. Who was Max shocked to see at the Refreshment Court?
16. What was the big event Max proposed to restore St Mary's prestige?
17. Where in the Cathedral were the documents that the Historians were planning to rescue?
18. What was the common theme of the three masterpieces saved from the Bonfire?
19. How had Mary Schiller died?
20. What did Sands take great delight in saying as they rescued Max and Leon?
21. Why did Isabella Barclay lie to Max about being her half-sister?
22. Who turned out to be the resident expert on the planned Thermopylae Jump?

Answers

1. Sinking Peterson's submarine
2. Hairpins and a stamp in the groin
3. In the priest hole
4. Edmund Lacey
5. Up in the attic
6. Touching her bonnet
7. The boys, James and Charles Lacey
8. Contemporary St Mary's
9. He landed in a laurel bush
10. Professor Eddie Penrose
11. Their muffs
12. A water jug, a window, the fruit bowl, and a pillow
13. To determine whether Sands was able to carry out a Historian's duties
14. Rosie Lee
15. Dr Bairstow, Annie Bessant, and Clive Ronan
16. Rescuing artworks from the Bonfire of the Vanities, Florence 1497
17. The Crypt
18. Paris of Troy
19. Shot through the forehead
20. Toc-Toc (Knock-knock)
21. So Max would walk away and she could shoot her in the back
22. Markham

Round Three

Questions

1. Who arrived early at 17th Century St Mary's?
2. What were the main differences between modern St Mary's and the 17th Century one?
3. Who played the role of 'the servant' who took young James Lacey to the village?
4. What were Schiller and Roberts keen to see at the Great Exhibition?
5. Why couldn't Max participate in the St Paul's assignment?
6. What was hidden in David Sands' walking cane?
7. Who did Max put in charge of the Great Fire of London Jump?
8. What was the bet on the outcome of the Boat Race between Max and Professor Penrose?
9. What had Evans superglued to his chest for the "Blood, Disease, and Torture" tour?
10. Who did Max suggest as the figurehead for the St Mary's boat?
11. Who gave the archery demonstration at the Open Day?
12. What was the name of the Thirsk raft for the boat race?
13. Who spoke perfect Italian and led the conversations in Florence?
14. What did Max invent to break the tension between her and Leon?
15. What did Peterson suggest to prevent Max being sent off to Thirsk for lighter duties?
16. Where did Max (foolishly) hide her chocolate stash?
17. Who did Leonidas send to block the goat track?
18. Who led the Persians over the mountain on the goat path?
19. What tactic did Leonidas use to break the Persian Immortals?
20. What happened to the missing set of desert camo fatigues?
21. Who accidentally knocked the bastard Ephialtes out with a rock?
22. What colour was Max's wedding dress?

Answers

1. Edmund Lacey
2. The chimneys, the roof, and the size
3. Peterson
4. The elephant
5. At that date she was already on the dodo hunt
6. A stun gun and some whisky
7. Van Owen and Schiller
8. Seven days of the loser's services for the winner
9. A stuffed rat called Archie
10. Kleio, the Muse of History
11. Peterson and Schiller
12. The Black Carbuncle
13. Sands
14. The Ta-dah Donut Challenge
15. That he and Max swap jobs
16. Under her pillow
17. His Phocian allies
18. Peterson
19. Appear to flee, then turn, and stab the disrupted pursuing enemy
20. Ephialtes had sloped off still wearing them. The bastard!
21. Markham
22. Gold

Round Four

Questions

1. Who founded St Mary's Priory in the late 13th Century?
2. Why was adultery practically the 17th Century national sport?
3. Which book did Markham accidentally reveal he had read?
4. What novel suggestion was mooted for car parking at the Open Day?
5. What did Henry of Rushford's granddaughter do to 14th Century St Mary's?
6. How could Max go back to St Paul's on the same day she was in Mauritius?
7. What did Max suspect was the reason for the good behaviour of the children at the Crystal Palace?
8. What was Max's bar nickname, of which she was previously unaware?
9. What was Clive Ronan's plan to get what he wanted with no one being killed?
10. What dreadful order had Dr Bairstow given Markham if Max was not in the pod by the appointed time?
11. What did Dr Bairstow want Professor Rapson to do for him?
12. Why did Leon think Max had died?
13. Where was David Sands at St Paul's?
14. Where did Dr Dowson propose concealing the rescued artworks?
15. What was David Sands' punishment for his sarcastic comment during the Open Day briefing?
16. What did Max plan to name her hypothetical town centre house?
17. Who shot Isabella Barclay?
18. Where did Max keep her secret margaritas?
19. What ended Max and Leon's row in the Florence storeroom?
20. What book did Markham reveal he had read when they were at Thermopylae?
21. What did one of the Spartan scouts do to Max?
22. What immortal words did Peterson spray paint on the cliff behind Leonidas' head?

Answers

1. Augustinian monks
2. There was no organised football yet
3. Jane Eyre
4. Free to enter, pay to leave
5. Tried to burn it down
6. If she left before 11.30, thirty minutes before she arrived on Mauritius
7. The huge quantity of clothing weighing them down
8. The Margarita Monster
9. Take Annie and walk away
10. Shoot her, to prevent there being two instances of the same person at the same time
11. Make him a cane like Sands'
12. She missed lunch
13. Unconscious on the floor of Number Eight
14. The Belverde caves, near Monte Cetona
15. 'Volunteering' to clean up the day after
16. Sea View
17. Greta van Owen
18. In an empty bubble bath bottle
19. He proposed
20. Wuthering Heights
21. Peed on her
22. "Go tell the Spartans, stranger passing by, that here, obedient to their laws, we lie"

Notes

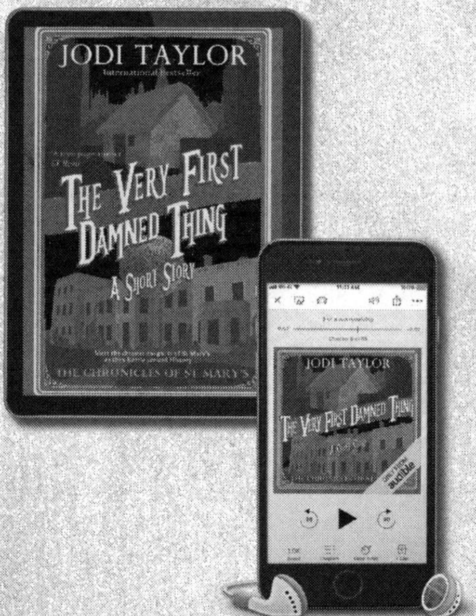

The Very First Damned Thing

It's two years since the final victory at the Battersea Barricades. The fighting might be finished, but for Dr Bairstow, just now setting up St Mary's, the struggle is only beginning.

How will he assemble his team?

How does stolen furniture, a jump to the Stirrup Charge at Waterloo, students' alcohol-ridden urine, a widowed urban guerrilla, a young man wearing exciting knitwear, and four naked security guards all combine to become the St Mary's of the future?

Questions

1. What are the only three things more important in the history of mankind than Dr Bairstow's meeting with the panel?
2. According to the sign over the door, what was the business Dr Bairstow was visiting?
3. What was Dr Chalfont's new role?
4. What did Dr Bairstow say was the use of time travel?
5. What information did Dr Bairstow say he could not provide?
6. Where did Dr Bairstow propose to take the panel?
7. Which specific part of the battle did the panel get to see?
8. What kept the pod safe from cannon fire?
9. Who banged on the pod door?
10. Who was the first person to be recruited by Dr Bairstow?
11. What was Major Guthrie's' only condition on coming to work for Dr Bairstow?
12. What was Markham's first action on entering St Mary's?
13. What was the first success of the Resistance?
14. What was the problem with the students' urine that caused things to explode?
15. What was Theresa Mack's only decoration in her room?
16. Where did Markham source the furniture for St Mary's?
17. What cake did Evelyn Chalfont's brightly painted mini resemble?
18. Who was Mrs Green?
19. Why had Mrs Partridge not come in answer to the advert for a PA?
20. Which organisation had Miss Spindle left SPOHB to work for?
21. Who was the seventh and last person on Dr Bairstow's list?
22. Where was the Very First Assignment?

Answers

1. The discovery of fire, the development of the wheel, and the invention of chocolate
2. Britannic Enterprises
3. Chancellor at the University of Thirsk
4. To record the actual truth of events
5. Whether the Uprisings and the Civil War would ever happen again
6. Waterloo 1815
7. The 92nd Highlanders and Scots Greys stirrup charge
8. Sturdy construction, careful choice of landing site, and the protection of the god of Historians
9. Max, Bashford, and Markham
10. Mr Strong
11. That he could bring his own team, including Markham, with him
12. Put the kettle on
13. Throwing the Fascists out of Cardiff
14. It was about 90% alcohol
15. A photograph of her and her husband
16. The local municipal tip
17. Battenberg
18. Angela Bessant
19. Dr Bairstow hadn't placed it yet
20. A male modelling agency
21. Leon
22. Julius Caesar's landing in the south of Britain, 55BC

Notes

What Could Possibly Go Wrong?

With great privilege comes great responsibility, something Max knows only too well, and as newly appointed Chief Training Officer at the St Mary's Institute of Historical Research, it's up to her to drum this guiding principle into her five new recruits.

Expect a training programme that includes Joan of Arc, an illegal mammoth, a duplicitous Father of History, a bombed rat, Stone Age hunters and Dick the Turd.

Round One

Questions

1. Name the new History Department recruits?
2. What was the new trainees' first assignment?
3. What new role is Max given after returning from Honeymoon?
4. What disturbed Max and Peterson's quiet drink?
5. What natural disaster nearly wrecks the Valley of the Kings Jump?
6. What did Sykes and Lingoss use to try to deal with the rat?
7. Who is Max's PA?
8. Where was the trainees' next assignment?
9. Which horse did Max recommend the trainees to learn to ride on?
10. What was the discovery made at the campsite?
11. What were the prehistoric humans hunting?
12. What did the hunters herd the mammoths towards?
13. What did the trainees bring back from the Palaeolithic?
14. How did Max create a diversion in Thurii?
15. What tried and tested St Mary's method did the trainees use to get out of the prison building?
16. What did North see herself doing in five years' time?
17. Who went into the well to rescue the little boy?
18. What was the trainees' Violent Death assignment?
19. Where did Hoyle want to Jump to?
20. Who turned up after the execution?
21. What life changing news did Helen have for Max?
22. Where was the trainees' final training Jump?

Answers

1. Lingoss, Sykes, North, Atherton, Hoyle
2. To survey and map the Valley of the Kings
3. Chief Training Officer
4. A massive explosion
5. Flash flood
6. Molotov cocktails
7. Rosie Lee
8. The Pleistocene Ice Age
9. Turk
10. Neanderthals and Cro-Magnon humans cohabited
11. Mammoths
12. Pits
13. A baby mammoth
14. Hip-bumped Herodotus into a market stall
15. They set it on fire
16. Max's job
17. Leon
18. The execution of Joan of Arc
19. The Battle of Bosworth Field, 1485
20. The Time Police
21. She was pregnant
22. To the opening of the Clifton Suspension Bridge, Bristol, 1864

Round Two

Questions

1. Who kept Randall alive under the floodwater?
2. What was the most baffling part about the new intake of trainees for Max?
3. How did the team defeat the sabre-toothed tigers?
4. What was Hoyle's area of speciality?
5. Who did Max suggest sending as the St Mary's representative to the Belverde caves to witness the unearthing of the lost Botticellis?
6. Who slipped and twisted their ankle just before the Egyptian storm?
7. Why were no qualified Historians required for the trainee's second Jump?
8. Why was Helen Foster so bad-tempered?
9. What effect did the Sonic Scream have on Max?
10. Who blamed Herodotus for ruining her perfect assignment?
11. What did Herodotus ask for?
12. What skill did Markham try to teach Peterson while he was still in Sick Bay?
13. How did Herodotus get the trainees arrested?
14. What foreign object prevented Emergency Extraction?
15. Who went out of the pod intending to give Joan of Arc a quick clean death?
16. Who did Ellis warn Max to keep an eye on?
17. What was Hoyle's plan?
18. Who threw the knife that killed Randall out of the pod?
19. Who had Hoyle always reminded Max of?
20. Why do female Historians usually take a wicker basket with them on Jumps?
21. Who did Hoyle threaten to shoot to make Max Jump to an unknown destination?
22. What did Sykes and Markham paint in a certain Leicester car park?

Answers

1. Sykes
2. One of them was from America, but not American
3. Rape alarm, blasters, and the sonic scream
4. The Wars of the Roses and the Tudor succession
5. Elspeth Grey
6. Sands
7. It was an observe and record mission only, with no interaction
8. She was trying to give up smoking
9. Nausea, dizziness, and disorientation
10. North
11. A ciggy
12. One-handed bra unfastening
13. He told the local police equivalent that they stole something from him
14. A knife stuck in Randall's ribs
15. Randall
16. Hoyle
17. To shoot Henry Tudor (or his horse)
18. North
19. Richard III
20. It gave them something to do with their hands, and could conceal contraband tea, chocolate, and stun guns
21. Markham
22. The Letter R

Round Three

Questions

1. Why did TB2 have to Jump away from the Valley of the Kings?
2. What was Max's plan for any trainee unable to hack their baby Jumps?
3. What did Peterson say everyone would call Miss Lingoss?
4. What was the most jarring thing about Hoyle?
5. What was bothering North about the trainees' first Jump?
6. Who were Bashford and Prentiss going to 11th Century Coventry to see?
7. Whose feet suffered from Professor Rapson's experimental heat exchanger boots?
8. Who hadn't fought at the Battle of St Mary's?
9. What was the most important thing to remember on a Jump to Hastings in 1066?
10. What was Elspeth's biggest issue after being missing for ten years?
11. What worrying conclusion had Markham come to about the St Paul's disaster?
12. How did the trainees get the mammoth out of Hawking?
13. What new, high-tech feature caused all the excitement in Number Five?
14. What finally stopped North from beating Herodotus to a pulp?
15. Where did the Historians leave the baby Mammoth?
16. Who was in Prentiss' warming pan?
17. Why did Lingoss want to switch from History to R&D?
18. What was Rosie Lee's reaction to finding out there was a mole at St Mary's?
19. Why was Rosie Lee crying?
20. Who threw Rosie Lee's hairdryer out of the window?
21. What happened to Hoyle?
22. What 'Thank you' gift did the trainees get Max?

Answers

1. It was blocking the flash flood that would carry hundreds of tons of mud and debris into the Valley that would eventually cover and protect Tutankhamen's tomb
2. Tie a brick around their neck and throw them into the lake
3. Connie
4. He didn't like tea
5. She wasn't in charge
6. Lady Godiva
7. Bashford
8. Mr Swanson, practically blind, Mrs Midgely in Sick Bay, Rosie Lee
9. Don't look up
10. Major Guthrie wasn't the same person she remembered
11. Someone inside St Mary's tipped off Clive Ronan
12. On a flatbed trolley, covered in a blanket
13. Cupholders
14. The tray fell apart
15. The Pleistocene Park
16. A very cross Vortigern
17. History wasn't 'interesting' enough for her
18. That "we" had a problem
19. She'd had a falling out with David Sands
20. Sands
21. Trampled to death by a horse
22. Membership of the Chocolate Association

Round Four

Questions

1. Who did Randall offer to do to North's boots to soften them up?
2. When Max was outlining the different colours of the sections, what did she say R&D wore?
3. Why couldn't Markham go to Thurii with them?
4. Who was the only person at St Mary's who didn't seem to like Peterson?
5. What did Dr Bairstow decide to do about the fake Herodotus?
6. What was the real, if unofficial, reason for the 100 year rule?
7. According to Leon, what's quicker and easier than arguing with Max?
8. What did Leon ask of Max?
9. How did Max effortlessly complete the Outdoor survival exercise?
10. What did 'consult as widely as you like' mean for the trainees?
11. Why did the trainees go to the River Medway in AD884?
12. What did Professor Rapson ask if Lingoss had on her?
13. Who had betrayed St Mary's to Clive Ronan?
14. What did Max suspect Herodotus had done with the contemporary whose clothes he stole?
15. Why did North despise Henry Tudor?
16. Why had Lingoss left a dead pig in the car park space next to Dr Bairstow's Bentley?
17. What book did Markham reveal he had read this time?
18. How did Clive Ronan blackmail Randall?
19. What was the latest fashionable Victorian colour?
20. What did everyone do to get the smell of charred flesh out of their noses?
21. Why did Max assure Hoyle she wouldn't make any sudden moves?
22. What was Hoyle's full name?

Answers

1. Pee on them
2. Protective clothing, wound dressings, and dazed expressions
3. Allergic reaction to something
4. Rosie Lee
5. Tell the Time Police about him and let them sort it out
6. Dr Bairstow wouldn't let anyone go back and annoy Stephen Hawking
7. Eating your own legs
8. Not to return to her old job for six months
9. Hitched two lifts and got a taxi
10. That they could ask anyone as many questions as they wanted
11. To watch the Vikings sail out of the mist to attack Rochester
12. A crochet hook
13. Randall
14. Killed him
15. He sent his men forward while he stayed safely in the rear
16. The disabled space was occupied
17. The Hound of the Baskervilles
18. He found out that Randall and some friends beat someone up so badly he was paralysed
19. Purple
20. Dab menthol on their upper lip
21. She was wearing a crinoline - no one could make sudden moves in one of them
22. Richard Neville Laurence Hoyle

Notes

Ships and Stings and Wedding Rings

It's Christmas at St Mary's and time for Max's obligatory illegal jump. On this occasion, however, they're right up against it.

A loaded gun has been left behind in Ancient Egypt and it's up to them to retrieve it before anyone accidentally blows their own head off, thus affecting the timeline for centuries to come.

And as if that's not enough, someone (Max) has inadvertently poisoned Mr Markham.

It's hot, they're running out of supplies, they can't find the gun, and it's all going horribly wrong. Again.

Questions

1. What aspect of Egyptian culture did Grey, Bashford, Cox, and Gallaccio jump to study?
2. What did Grey lose on the assignment?
3. Who came third in the Security Section's Annual All Comers One Handed Bra Unfastening Competition?
4. What did Markham use to fuse the Security Section's monitors?
5. Whose makeshift costume and makeup made him look like a grumpy transvestite?
6. What sacred symbol was the stern post of the ship carved into?
7. What are the three tourist traditions when visiting Egypt?
8. What did the older boy get from the trader for the gun?
9. What did Max have to pay to get the gun back?
10. What had Max been spraying Markham with for days?
11. Why did Markham get an extra seven days in Sick Bay?
12. What did Leon give Max for Christmas?

Answers

1. Shipbuilding
2. A handgun
3. Peterson
4. Fairy lights
5. Markham's
6. A lotus flower
7. See the pyramids, get ripped off, throw up
8. A clump round the head
9. Her wedding ring
10. WD40
11. He'd been dunked in, and swallowed, the filthy waters of the Nile
12. Her wedding ring

Notes

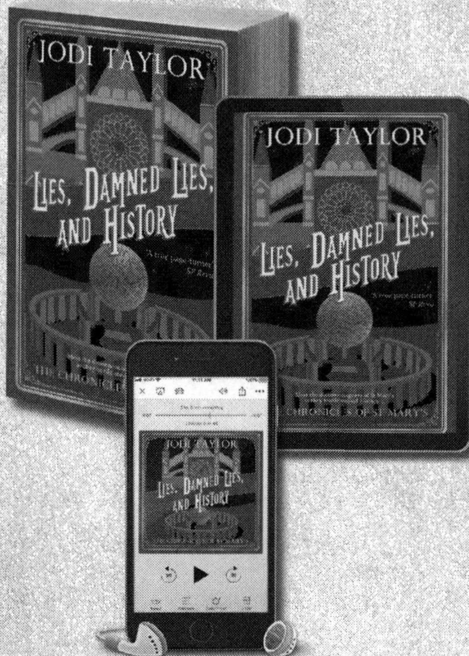

Lies, Damned Lies, and History

Max has never been one for rules. They tend to happen to other people.

But this time she's gone too far. And everyone at St Mary's is paying the price.

With the History Department disintegrating around her and grounded until the end of time, how can she ever put things right?

Round One

Questions

1. Who lost part of their ear in the William Tell emulation?
2. What customary injury did Bashford suffer on the Arminius Jump?
3. What nickname did Max give to Arminius?
4. Who was the first royal to arrive at the coronation?
5. Where was King George to be crowned?
6. What did the King give to the druid?
7. What went wrong with the simple 'observe and record' mission at the Coronation?
8. Who comforted Markham?
9. Who came to the rescue of the villagers at the hill fort?
10. What had Sykes, Bashford, and Lingoss done?
11. Where was the peaceful hill fort Max was assigned to map?
12. Why did Halcombe order the Emergency Extraction?
13. How had Sands presented his report of Viking life in Jorvik?
14. To which event did Halcombe insist on leading the Jump?
15. After the theft from Thirsk University, who takes over as Jump supervisor?
16. Where did Max want to make an illicit Jump to?
17. Where was Max's last Jump going to be?
18. What did Markham know about the weather on Salisbury Plain?
19. Who was waiting for Max outside the back door?
20. Which familiar face rescued Max?
21. What name do Max & Leon give their son?
22. Where did Clive Ronan take Max?

Answers

1. Markham
2. Blow to the head and concussion
3. Herman the German
4. Caroline of Brunswick, the Queen
5. Westminster Abbey
6. A sword
7. Max dropped her recorder
8. Hunter
9. King Arthur Pendragon
10. Got themselves arrested
11. Caer Guorthigirn
12. He thought he'd been jostled by a leper
13. In the form of a Norse saga
14. The presentation of Edward, the first Prince of Wales to the Welsh population
15. Malcolm Halcombe
16. The Wash, October 1216
17. To Stonehenge, 2600BC
18. It's always raining
19. Clive Ronan
20. Captain Ellis
21. Matthew
22. Some unknown, unnamed, desolate place

Round Two

Questions

1. Where did the entire hill fort population go the next morning?
2. How did the Saxons intend to get the women and children out of the storehouse?
3. What colour cloak did the King wear to denote royalty?
4. Who was taken off by the hill fort guards?
5. What was the King's banner?
6. Who went off to Thirsk to be the St Mary's representative on the sword recovery assignment?
7. Who did Max insist that everybody had to say was responsible the theft?
8. Who resigned, taking all the blame for the theft as far as the outside world was concerned?
9. Who arrested the thieves when they returned to St Mary's?
10. Who caused widespread panic by getting off the car roof while made up as a two-day-dead corpse?
11. What were Bashford, Sykes, and Lingoss arrested for?
12. Who fetched Malcolm Halcombe his coffee?
13. How did Markham dismissively refer to Halcombe?
14. Who seemed to be the only injured party on the Caernarfon Jump?
15. What disturbed Max's lunch?
16. How did Lingoss stun the Caernarfon crowd?
17. Who blackmailed their way onto the Wash Jump?
18. What destroyed the baggage train?
19. Why did Peterson want Max to close her eyes while he Jumped the pod to Stonehenge?
20. Who had a brilliant idea at The Wash?
21. Why was Max happy to see a tree up on the rocky hillside?
22. Who rescued them all from the Salisbury Plain snowstorm?

Answers

1. Arthur's Cave
2. Burn them out
3. Blue
4. Peterson, Markham, Roberts, and Sands
5. A red dragon on a gold background
6. Elspeth Grey
7. Herself
8. Roberts and Sands
9. Major Guthrie
10. Bashford
11. Transporting a dead body
12. Rosie Lee
13. "Coffee drinker"
14. North
15. The crash of a pod undergoing Emergency Extraction
16. Took off her hat to show her Mohican
17. Dottle
18. A storm surge
19. So the first thing she would see would be dawn rising over the stones
20. Peterson
21. Trees need water, there had to be a stream or spring there
22. Leon

Round Three

Questions

1. Why did Peterson say the guards gave Roberts a stick, not a sword?
2. What happened to Queen Caroline after the Coronation?
3. What was the first thing to go wrong after the sword was recovered?
4. Where did Max and the others hide the sword?
5. What disaster affected Roberts' family farm?
6. Who was fired after defending St Mary's over the sword?
7. What finally convinced the Historians that they had a problem?
8. What was Max's job until she gave birth?
9. As an expert criminal, what did Markham insist they planned first?
10. What was Leon's suggested face-saving gesture?
11. Who did Halcombe order the Historians to leave behind?
12. How did they get through the keypad security system at Thirsk?
13. How did Max keep Halcombe under wraps while she rescued the abandoned people?
14. What did Max try to bribe the police sergeant to do?
15. Where did they Jump to, so they could rob the baggage train before it was lost in The Wash?
16. What then did Max offer, which got them released?
17. Who did Max see in her Stonehenge dream?
18. What important question did only Dottle ask about Caernarfon?
19. Why did Clive Ronan take Max somewhere out of her own time to give birth?
20. Who Jumped to Caernarfon to bring back the abandoned Historians?
21. Who fired a fizzer into the air to alert Max that they had arrived?
22. What did they find was going on in the dark in Bishop's Lynn?

Answers

1. They thought he was a girl because he didn't have a beard
2. She fell ill and died (or was she poisoned?)
3. A local factory closure
4. Down Markham's trousers
5. Foot and mouth
6. Dr Chalfont, the Chancellor of Thirsk University
7. An archaeological trench collapsed, killing one of the Thirsk academics
8. Fund raising ideas
9. Their getaway
10. Rent a cottage in the village, and Max could start her maternity leave immediately
11. Bashford, Sykes, and Dottle
12. Markham memorised the tune of the correct key sequence
13. Told Helen to quarantine him for suspected leprosy
14. Keep the Historians locked up forever
15. Bishop's Lynn
16. To take them away and have them shot
17. Herne and the Wild Hunt
18. Did Edward I present his new-born son as the Prince of Wales?
19. Because then her baby would never be able to leave that time
20. Max, Markham, Evans, and Lingoss
21. The Time Police
22. King John was stealing his own treasure

Round Four

Questions

1. Why was George IV late for his own coronation?
2. Which famous bare-knuckle boxer had the King employed to keep his wife from the coronation?
3. What did Max contribute to the communal meal at Caer Guorthigirn?
4. What intriguing item of kit did Arthur and his men use, that Max failed to recognise as important?
5. How did the male Historians avoid accidentally killing any contemporaries at the battle of Caer Guorthigirn?
6. How were the other thieves punished?
7. Where did Dr Dowson find space for Max to work?
8. How was Max determined to rub everyone's noses in it?
9. When Max needed to leave St Mary's, which member of Senior Staff did she go to for permission?
10. What precisely set off the alarm at Thirsk?
11. What did Halcombe incorrectly accuse Max of doing?
12. What question did Dr Bairstow carefully NOT ask after the theft?
13. How did Max placate the Caernarfon fishwife?
14. What did the sergeant request that Max do with the Historians?
15. Who did Peterson say should be the discoverer of any rescued items?
16. What argument caused the Caernarfon pub riot?
17. What were prowling around in the forest while Max and Peterson were burying the treasures?
18. What did Max think was a sign of Leon's sick mind?
19. What new parasite had made its home inside Markham?
20. What did Peterson and Markham manage to steal from the Crown Jewels?
21. Once again, Markham revealed he'd read another literary classic. Which one?
22. Who did Dr Bairstow suspect were behind Halcombe?

Answers

1. He tore something, and had to re-dress
2. Gentleman' John Jackson
3. The despised high-energy biscuits
4. Stirrups
5. They fought each other
6. Demoted, and required to witness the results of their actions
7. In the Cretan Pottery section of the Archive
8. Being the best fundraiser in the history of the world, ever
9. Professor Rapson
10. Touching the sword
11. Going outside the grounds without permission
12. "What did you do with the sword"
13. Showed her pregnant belly and gave her a flatfish
14. Take them away and drown them
15. Dr Chalfont
16. Either a daughter or a horse
17. Wolves
18. He squeezed toothpaste tubes from the bottom
19. Ringworm
20. Empress Mathilda's crown, and the Sword of Tristram
21. A Tale of Two Cities
22. The same people who had been behind Hoyle

Notes

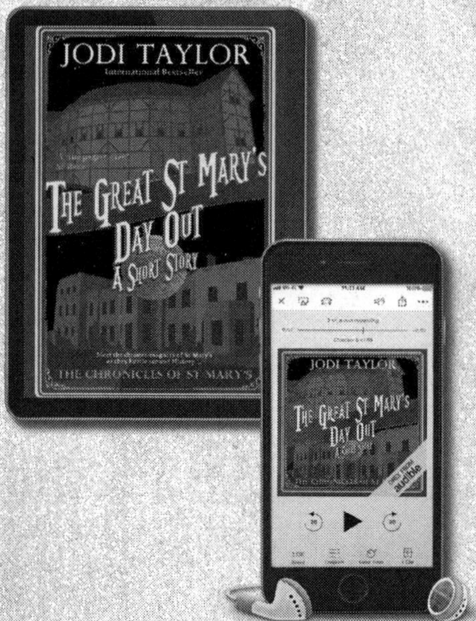

THE GREAT ST MARY'S DAY OUT

Astonishingly, Dr Bairstow has declared a holiday. Even more astonishingly - he's paying for it.

Needless to say, there are strings attached. They have to record the 1601 performance of Hamlet, with Shakespeare himself in the role of the Ghost.

It doesn't go well, of course. With Dr Bairstow and Mrs Mack turning a simple visit to a street market into a public brawl, Professor Rapson inadvertently stowing away on a vessel bound for the New World, and Shakespeare himself going up in flames, it would seem that Max, of all people, is the only one actually completing the assignment.

Questions

1. Where was the Big Day Out going to be?
2. Where did TB2 land?
3. Which pub did Max's team head for on arrival?
4. How much were the posh seats at the Globe?
5. What had happened to Professor Rapson?
6. Who started a small riot by refusing to acquiesce to having their pocket picked?
7. How long a play was Hamlet?
8. Which role was William Shakespeare playing?
9. What potential disaster occurred?
10. Who took over the role of The Ghost?
11. What is St Mary's code for "It's all going tits up"?
12. What was Miss Sykes whispered nickname?
13. What did Markham bribe the understudy with?

Answers

1. The Globe Theatre, London, June 1601, to see Hamlet
2. At the Bear Garden on Bankside
3. The Tabard
4. 6d
5. Stuck on a ship destined for the New World
6. Mrs Mack
7. Four hours
8. The Ghost
9. Shakespeare's costume caught on fire
10. Markham
11. Everything's fine
12. Psycho Psykes
13. A brick sized bar of fruit & nut

Notes

My Name is Markham

It's Christmas and time for the first (and almost certainly last) St Mary's Annual Children's Christmas Party - attendance compulsory, by order of Dr Bairstow. Discovered practising his illegal reindeer dance and poo-dropping routine, our hero, along with fellow disaster-magnets Peterson and Maxwell, is despatched to Anglo-Saxon England to discover the truth about Alfred and the cakes.

In his own words, our hero reveals Major Guthrie's six-point guide to a successful assignment and the Security Section's true opinion of the History Department. And of historians in general. And of one historian in particular.

Questions

1. What did Professor Rapson's artificial snow do?
2. How did Miss North offend Mrs Enderby and all of Wardrobe?
3. How did Dr Bairstow encourage Markham to accompany Max on her last assignment before Christmas?
4. What had the row at Thirsk been about?
5. What did Max wear under her dress?
6. Where was the jump to?
7. What was Max wearing on her feet?
8. What did every hunter, fisherman, and herdsman bring back to the village?
9. Who gave Alfred their beer?
10. How did the fire go out?
11. How did Markham relight the fire?
12. What did Markham do to create a diversion?
13. What music had Markham chosen for the reindeer dance routine?
14. Who was the front end of the reindeer?
15. Who burnt the cakes?

Answers

1. Set fire to the workbench
2. Hired a Snow Queen costume
3. Tearing up a pile of Deductions from Wages forms
4. Whether or not the cakes had been burned
5. Anomalous underwear
6. Isle of Athelney, Somerset, 878 AD
7. Gryffindor rugby socks
8. Firewood
9. Markham
10. One of the lustful dogs knocked a pan of water into it
11. With a blaster. On full power
12. Set off a fizzer
13. The Can-can
14. Evans
15. Markham

Notes

And The Rest is History

When an old enemy appears out of nowhere with an astonishing proposition for Max - a proposition that could change everything - Max is tempted. Very tempted.

With an end to an old conflict finally in sight, it looks as if St Mary's problems are over with. Can they all now live happily ever after?

But as everything hangs in the balance, Max and St Mary's find themselves engulfed in tragedies worse than they could ever imagine.

Is this the end?

Round One

Questions

1. Why had Max and Leon stayed at St Mary's?
2. What wiped out Cambyses' army?
3. What had Peterson recently accomplished?
4. What two things did Leon promise Max?
5. Who had a crush on Peterson?
6. What was Max's biggest success with Matthew's new clothes?
7. Where did Clive Ronan's coordinates lead to?
8. Which four Jumps had been planned for the History department?
9. Who did Dieter say had worms?
10. What did Max use to take away Matthew's nightmares?
11. Where was Max when approached by Clive Ronan?
12. Who came to see Max and Matthew late one night, cold and wet from a snowstorm?
13. Who did Clive Ronan shoot when he returned to St Mary's?
14. What proposition did Commander Hay have for Max and Matthew?
15. What reappearance in the sky did both Saxons and Normans see as a bad omen?
16. What gentle leisure activity did Dr Bairstow propose as a celebratory event to commemorate the completion of Hawking's repairs?
17. What appeared on the South Lawn in the middle of afternoon tea?
18. What news had Commander Hay brought?
19. Who wrote out Peterson's speech and question for him?
20. What were the last known coordinates of the missing St Mary's personnel?
21. Who disrupted Max and Peterson's date?
22. Who did the Constantinople searchers find first?

Answers

1. For fear of another kidnapping attempt
2. A giant sandstorm
3. Persuaded Helen Foster to marry him
4. To bring Matthew home in two days, and to shoot Clive Ronan dead
5. Dottle
6. His light-up trainers
7. The Egyptian desert, 525BC
8. Harold's shipwreck and handover to William, Harold's oath, the Battle of Stamford Bridge, and the Battle of Hastings
9. Markham
10. A projection copy of the Time Map
11. Jogging round the lake
12. Leon, from before his death
13. Helen
14. That he lived at Time Police Headquarters and was educated there
15. Halley's Comet
16. Croquet on the lawn, in period costume
17. A giant teapot
18. Clive Ronan had escaped, and Major Guthrie, Leon, Markham, and Van Owen might still be alive
19. Kal
20. Constantinople, April 1204
21. The Time Police
22. Markham

Round Two

Questions

1. What interrupted Max in the desert?
2. How long did the Persian army take to pass?
3. Which members of the Time Police arrived in Dr Bairstow's office?
4. What did Peterson put on Helen's coffin?
5. Who, surprisingly, brought Max some lunch after Matthew's abduction?
6. What happened to Helen's lighter?
7. Which previous Historian had now joined the Time Police?
8. What was Dr Bairstow's concern for Matthew's future?
9. Where did William's forces land?
10. What had Max forgotten for the first time in her life?
11. Which of Matthew's toys did not go with him to Time Police Headquarters?
12. Who did Matthew become the devoted slave of?
13. How long did Dr Bairstow ask Max to stay at St Mary's before leaving and setting up home with Matthew?
14. How did Dr Stone get Max to come for an eye test?
15. Why could Adrian and Mikey only stay for 2 hours?
16. Who invaded the North of England in 1066?
17. What did Matthew tell Max about Leon?
18. Who triggered the Norman cavalry's fall into the Malfosse ditch?
19. What was absent from the Time Police's London?
20. What did Max see out of Dr Bairstow's window while briefing him on the Stamford Bridge Jump?
21. Who did the wall fall on top of in Constantinople?
22. What was Max was horrified to learn was rationed in the future?

Answers

1. A flash of light in the distance
2. Nearly two hours
3. Commander Hay, and Captains Ellis and Farenden
4. A red rose, a packet of cigarettes, and a box of matches
5. Rosie Lee
6. Peterson kept it
7. Greta Van Owen
8. Lack of socialisation with other children
9. Pevensey
10. To eat
11. His blue teddy bear
12. Lingoss
13. Six months
14. Blackmailed her with a psych test
15. Because that's generally when the Time Police showed up
16. Tostig of Northumberland and Harald Hardrada of Norway
17. "He's not near the others"
18. Max and Evans
19. Cars
20. A dachshund cartwheeling through the sky
21. Max
22. Tea

ROUND THREE

Questions

1. What was the first evidence of the Persian Army seen by Max and Clive Ronan?
2. How many tags did Max have now after Clive Ronan's last kidnap attempt?
3. What had Max concealed about her person to disable Clive Ronan's pod?
4. How many Time Police does it take to subdue one small Historian?
5. Who did Dr Bairstow appoint as the new Medical Officer?
6. How old did the Matthew that Leon brought back look?
7. What was Leon's only complaint about Matthew's new light-up trainers?
8. Where had the new Medical Officer been before St Mary's?
9. How did William trick Harold?
10. How was the next King after the childless Edward the Confessor determined?
11. How did Harold win Norman hearts and minds?
12. While in Count Guy's castle, who poured Harold's wine?
13. How did Harald Hardrada die?
14. Where did Harold take his oath to support William's claim to the English throne?
15. Who did Clive Ronan mean by 'three birds with one stone'?
16. What relation was Bishop Odo of Conteville to King William?
17. Why would a dog fall from the sky and stun Bashford?
18. Why did women bow to King William?
19. What was wrong with 13th Century Constantinople?
20. Why did the Vikings leave their armour with their ships?
21. What did Max have to admit she liked about the Time Police?
22. Who else died in the blast of Clive Ronan's attack?

Answers

1. Two scout chariots
2. Three
3. An EMP device
4. Six
5. Dr Nathaniel Stone
6. Five or six
7. Max hadn't bought him a pair as well
8. In the Army
9. He concealed a saint's bones inside the altar on which Harold swore
10. By the Witan
11. Rescuing two Norman soldiers from quicksand
12. William
13. An arrow in the throat
14. Bayeaux Cathedral
15. Leon, Major Guthrie, and Max
16. Half-brother
17. Who else would it stun?
18. The curtsey hadn't been invented yet
19. The Crusaders were invading and burning everything
20. It was very hot, and Harold was almost 200 miles away
21. Their armour
22. Markham and Van Owen

Round Four

Questions

1. Who had taken Harold Godwinson into custody?
2. What game were Leon and Matthew playing in the bath?
3. What was the only damage or injury sustained in the first 1066 Jump?
4. In a crisis, people have the choice of Fight or Flight. What did Dr Bairstow say was the third choice?
5. What did the Bayeaux teams get Max as a gift to say sorry?
6. Who surprised Max by volunteering to go with Major Guthrie and Leon to hunt down Clive Ronan?
7. How did the Saxons kill the Viking giant on the bridge?
8. How many people survived Harold's shipwreck?
9. Where did Lingoss get all the stuffed animals?
10. What deceased animals did Professor Rapson request?
11. What was the name of the Yorkshire terrier that sailed through Dr Bairstow's window?
12. Who were Harold's brothers, caught and trampled by Norman cavalry?
13. What did Dr Stone want to do to Peterson?
14. What was SPOHB's BDSM department?
15. What special interest did the Time Police have in Matthew?
16. What was the final score of the croquet tournament?
17. Why was Max relieved that the Teapot had no safety protocols?
18. What did Max threaten a disobedient Matthew with?
19. Which two young Time Police Officers were assigned to babysit Matthew?
20. Which metaphysical poet did Markham reveal he had read at school?
21. How did Ellis reassure Max that Markham was still alive?
22. Who accidentally revealed she was pregnant?

Answers

1. Guy of Ponthieu
2. Attack of the Deadly Flannels
3. Markham broke a cupholder
4. Freeze
5. Yellow roses and chocolate biscuits
6. Elspeth Grey
7. Floated a barrel underneath him, and attacked him from below
8. Eight
9. Job lot from a retiring taxidermist
10. Seven dogs, eleven cats, and a species of crocodile
11. Colin
12. Gyrth and Leofwine
13. Syringe his ears
14. Building Design and Site Management
15. He was born between times, in the middle of a Jump
16. Time Police 0, St Mary's 1, minor injuries 15-20
17. She could load it up with supplies and it could Jump with them onboard
18. In front of the whole security section, she would give him a big kiss, and call him Mummy's Special Little Soldier
19. Trent and Parrish (no relation, we assume)
20. John Donne
21. The medics wouldn't waste time working to save a dead man
22. Hunter

Notes

A Perfect Storm is only available in audio in the short story anthology *The Long and Short of It*

A PERFECT STORM

You don't have to travel through time to experience catastrophe on an epic scale, as the disaster-magnets from St Mary's are about to find out...

For Max, what starts off as a perfectly normal week is about to degenerate into a quagmire of egotistical film producers, monumental pub crawls, unsigned contracts, exploding rocks, Professor Rapson and his megaphone, the world's biggest bacon butty - and Angus - the third component of the most notorious love triangle since Menelaus, Paris and Whatshername - the one with the face they launched ships off.

A Perfect Storm of calamity, devastation and misfortune only ever encountered at St Mary's.

Questions

1. What was planned to celebrate Max and Markham's return to normal duties?
2. What was David Sands' new book about?
3. Why was Max convinced Sands' book was nothing like St Mary's?
4. Who was Calvin Cutter?
5. What costumes did the pub crawlers decide to wear?
6. Who defended Basford against a bunch of inebriated young men?
7. Who sorted the four trying to get through the front door simultaneously into single file?
8. What was Calvin Cutter doing that Dr Bairstow found so discourteous?
9. How did Max rattle Calvin Cutter?
10. What did Calvin Cutter want to talk to the BBC Wildlife Unit in Bristol about?
11. Which atrocious fake accent did Mrs Enderby adopt for meeting Calvin Cutter?
12. What did Max claim that R&D contained?
13. What did Max want Professor Rapson to set up?
14. What did Calvin Cutter dismiss all historical research as?
15. What happened to herons coming too close to the St Mary's goldfish pond?
16. What happens when you spray vinegar, sour wine, or coca cola onto white-hot rocks?
17. What happened to David Sands' manuscript?
18. Where did Bashford suggest Angus could sleep?
19. Why did Dr Bairstow allow Angus to remain at St Mary's?

Answers

1. A Pub Crawl
2. A bunch of highly competent scientists whizzing up and down the timeline
3. They used wrist devices, and were called St Christopher's. And never jumped to the wrong place, no one caught on fire, no one gets arrested, nor catches dysentery, nor has any inappropriate sex
4. A film director
5. Superheroes
6. Angus
7. Mrs Partridge
8. Constantly taking into his mobile headset
9. Every time he talked into his headset, she thanked him for agreeing such generous contract terms
10. Swans that roost in trees
11. An Irish brogue
12. Records, going back for decades
13. The Hannibal Barca fire-setting experiments
14. Dead stuff
15. They were dragged underwater by a couple of koi
16. They explode
17. Calvin Cutter got hold of it
18. On top of his wardrobe
19. She raised the average IQ of the History Department

Notes

CHRISTMAS PAST

The First Farrell Family Christmas.

Max, Leon and Matthew - together at last for Christmas at a time of conspicuous consumption, riotous misbehaviour and the traditional illegal Christmas jump. And this time, it's inter-generational.

Donning her unfamiliar mother hat, Max takes Matthew back to 19th century London, where they plan to deliver a parcel of Christmas cheer to his former friends, but find themselves confronting the terrifying Old Ma Scrope in the process.

'Tis the season to be jolly.

Questions

1. What Christmas decoration had been affixed to Vortigern?
2. Where was Max's safe place where she could guarantee no work was happening?
3. Rather than give the pods a thorough servicing, what holiday activity were Tech up to?
4. What had Mrs Midgely's best tablecloths previously been used for?
5. Why was Max worried about the Christmas crackers?
6. What were the names of Matthew's fellow climbing boys?
7. What name had Matthew been given by the Scropes?
8. What did Matthew want to do?
9. Why did Matthew insist he had to come with Max?
10. Who helped Max and Matthew smuggle their costumes and gifts down to Leon's pod?
11. How did Matthew dissuade the footpads from attacking them?
12. What did Max threaten Ma Scrope with?
13. What had Ma Scrope hidden everywhere in the house?
14. What were Matthew's final words before going to help with the Yule log?

Answers

1. A red tinsel bow
2. Her office
3. Building a life-sized mechanical Rudolph
4. Sails on Viking longboats
5. R&D made them
6. James (or Jamie) and Joshua
7. Joseph (or Joe)
8. Jump back and give the boys some food
9. She wouldn't know the way to the Scropes' house
10. Peterson and Markham
11. He said their boxes were for Ma Scrope
12. That Max would follow her into the next world and get her revenge
13. Money
14. "Mummy's *awesome*!"

Notes

An Argumentation of Historians

They say you shouldn't push your luck. Max gives her own luck a massive shove every day - and it's only a matter of time until luck pushes back...

January 1536 - the day of Henry VIII's infamous jousting accident. Historians from St Mary's are there in force, recording and documenting. And, arguing - obviously.

A chance meeting between Max and the Time Police leads to a plan of action to bring down Clive Ronan, once and for all.

Round One

Questions

1. Why did Max go for the horn-rimmed glasses?
2. What were St Mary's going to observe at Greenwich?
3. Who was the new Head of Security?
4. Which king were they supposed to observe at the Tournament?
5. What was Peterson's new role?
6. Why was Dottle crying?
7. Where did Angus sleep every night?
8. What was the Great Battering Ram Experiment supposed to determine?
9. How did Markham describe him, Max, and Peterson?
10. Who was inside the huge dress, and objected to being groped by the Time Police?
11. Where did the team plan to Jump to first?
12. What gave Max away to Clive Ronan?
13. What did the Time Police want to set up as bait for Clive Ronan?
14. What was William Hendred's role?
15. How did Dr Bairstow communicate with the Time Police in the future?
16. Who provided Max with a room to sleep in?
17. What turned up again just as the barn was collapsed?
18. What melee weapon was Max moderately proficient at using?
19. Who had been shot by the Time Police?
20. What was Margery Daw's occupation?
21. Where did Clive Ronan's goons abandon Max?
22. How did Max defend herself from onion man, the gate guard?
23. What language did Max use when she couldn't understand the gate guard?
24. Who were planning to seize St Mary's?
25. What alias did Max use while in 14th Century Rushford?
26. Where was Clive Ronan hiding?

Answers

1. They made her look both intelligent and sexy
2. A jousting tournament
3. Markham
4. Henry VIII
5. Deputy Director
6. Halcombe was coming back
7. On top of Bashford's wardrobe
8. Did castle gates open inwards or outwards
9. The Dream Team
10. Rosie Lee
11. Greenwich Palace, January 1536
12. She answered in English
13. Max
14. Marshall
15. Wrote them a letter
16. William Hendred
17. The giant teapot
18. A quarterstaff
19. Mikey
20. Washerwoman
21. Near 14th Century St Mary's
22. Kicked him in the shin
23. Latin
24. Guy and Jerald of Rushford
25. Joan of Rouen
26. On the roof

Round Two

Questions

1. Which was the only one of Henry VIII's wives that Max thought looked pretty?
2. What was the first event on the tournament programme?
3. What did Max think she heard during Henry's second joust?
4. What did Halcombe object to finding on his History department report?
5. Where did Max decide to set the trap for Clive Ronan?
6. What had the battering ram been named?
7. Where did Max intend to hide the real crown?
8. What favour did Major Guthrie ask of Max?
9. What was Halcombe's first shocking suggestion upon his unwelcome return to St Mary's?
10. What did Max recognise first in 14th Century St Mary's?
11. What was Dottle carrying when Max almost bumped in to her?
12. What was served for breakfast at 14th Century St Mary's?
13. What did Max carry as a disguise when walking around Persepolis?
14. Why was Max's social status so low in the 14th Century?
15. What had happened to break the siege?
16. What did Max know about how the siege of St Mary's would end?
17. What peculiar colour was Jerald's horse?
18. Who lit the fires in the stables and feed store?
19. Who took Max to Rushford market?
20. What did Max buy for William Hendred?
21. Who was waiting for Max in the hunting lodge?
22. Who kidnapped Max when she was out gathering firewood?
23. Who was working with Clive Ronan all along?
24. Why did Guy intend to hurt Max?
25. What was in the teddy?
26. Where on the roof was Dottle hiding?

Answers

1. Anne of Cleves
2. An archery tourney, King's men vs locals
3. A gunshot
4. Chicken poo
5. Persepolis
6. Grond
7. In a bin labelled 'Kitchen Waste' left by the back door
8. Tell Markham of her complete confidence in him
9. Excluding women from some Jumps
10. The church
11. An enormous pile of sandwiches
12. Porridge
13. An urn of oil
14. She had no husband, nor any male relatives
15. Someone had spoiled the well water with a dead cat
16. In fire
17. Yellow
18. Margery Daw
19. William Hendred
20. A pie
21. Guy and Jerald
22. Onion man
23. Dottle
24. To break William and to weaken Sir Hugh
25. A short-range recording and transmitting device
26. Behind a chimney

Round Three

Questions

1. What did Clive Ronan's men do to Max in Persepolis?
2. What did Markham change the Security Section callsign to?
3. How did Max briefly get away from Clive Ronan?
4. How did Max manage two different costumes at Persepolis?
5. How was Alexander's' companion, Ptolemy recognisable?
6. What was the recurring theme of Persepolis' artwork and decoration?
7. What job was Max first given at 14th Century St Mary's?
8. What advice did Max give her captors?
9. Who was Marjory's assistant?
10. Who owned St Mary's?
11. How did Margery deal with onion man and Jerald?
12. Who downgraded Max to the easier job of stacking hay in the cart?
13. What had William bought for Max?
14. When the invasion force was sighted, where did most of the villagers go?
15. How did Max make Guy think she had Jumped?
16. What was Max's plan to defeat Guy?
17. Who took Max back to 1400 St Mary's to say goodbye to William Hendred?
18. What mysterious excuse did Max give to go up to the bedroom alone?
19. What went wrong with Clerk, Prentiss, and Cox's Jump?
20. How did Max deter Guy from coming after her?
21. Where had the disastrous Jump been to?
22. Who found Max in the snow` in Medieval Rushford?
23. What did the urchin drop, and Max pick up?
24. Where was Max going when Clive Ronan's goons came back?
25. How did Max survive the fall off the roof?
26. Who did Dr Stone send for to get Max to talk about her ordeal?

Answers

1. Disabled her tags
2. Horse's Arse
3. A burning beam fell between them
4. A dull brown servant's linen chiton, and, when needed, a long vivid red and green noblewoman's silk stole worn like a scarf
5. He was wearing the courtesan Thaïs like a rash
6. Conquered peoples bringing tribute
7. Hay raking
8. "Don't go back to Clive Ronan, he's going to kill you"
9. Little Alice
10. Sir Hugh Armstrong
11. Knocked them out with a wooden bucket
12. William Hendred
13. Some blue and green ribbons
14. Into the woods
15. Wrapped the bolster in her dress and cloak and threw it out of the window
16. Pretend to surrender, get them drunk, then burn St Mary's down around them
17. Leon
18. "Women's things"
19. There was a fight, and none of them will ever work with the others again
20. Set fire to the bolster underneath the window
21. Rushford, 1815, post-Waterloo
22. William and Tam
23. A pocketbook
24. To deliver Father and Rowena their basket of food
25. She grabbed at branches to slow her descent
26. Kalinda

Round Four

Questions

1. How did the Time Police know of the assassin's plans?
2. How did Max describe Dr Stone?
3. Who had been the assassin's intended target?
4. Which two graves at St Mary's upset Max the most?
5. What actually was Max going to use as bait for Clive Ronan?
6. Who was trying to persuade Alexander to burn Persepolis?
7. As well as revenge, what else did Max think was best served cold?
8. What finishing touch to TB2's disguise did Dr Stone object to?
9. Whose was the terrible scream that everyone ignored?
10. What was the danger with medieval bread?
11. What was the problem with the towels?
12. Who had just returned from France at the end of the 14th Century and would overthrow Richard II?
13. Who featured in Calvin Cutter's latest venture into historical fiction?
14. Who was William Hendred's second in command?
15. Who was the steward at medieval St Mary's?
16. How did the returned Sir Hugh reward Walter and William?
17. Why did Max tell Clive Ronan's young goon not to shoot her in the pod?
18. What did Sir Hugh give Max and Margery?
19. What was Max's next job, another downgrade?
20. What had happened to Clive Ronan's goons?
21. When Max woke up after coming back from Rushford, who stepped out of the locker?
22. What did Georgian Rushford mostly smell of?
23. What did Max suggest doing with Dottle's body?
24. How long was Max in the cell in Rushford before Leon could get her out?
25. How did Max realise something was wrong with the fifth Time Police Officer?
26. Who escorted the Time Police to take Dottle away?

Answers

1. He wrote to his girlfriend and boasted about them
2. Dr Devious, from Devioustown, in Deviousshire
3. Henry's unnamed opponent in the list
4. Helen Foster and Madeleine Maxwell
5. Empress Mathilda's Crown
6. Thaïs
7. Her feet in the middle of the night
8. A dead dog
9. Mrs Midgely's
10. Breaking a tooth on the grit in it
11. They contained a squished hamster
12. Henry Bolingbroke, Henry IV
13. Queen Elizabeth I
14. Tam the Welshman
15. Walter of Shrewsbury
16. One to be his Steward at the much larger Rushford Castle and estate, one to be the Lord of St Mary's
17. Because the bullet would go through her and damage the pod - and he'd have to carry her corpse outside, as well
18. A purse of coins to be a dowry for each of them
19. Hen heggler (egg collecting)
20. They had returned and Clive Ronan had shot them
21. Clive Ronan, holding baby Matthew
22. Tar
23. Leave it in the tree
24. Overnight
25. Time Police Squads are only four people
26. Evans

Round Five

Questions

1. What trick did the medieval people know to stop carp tasting of mud?
2. Why did Jane Seymour not get proper postnatal care?
3. What story did Max tell in the hall?
4. Which government-issued photo ID did Max possess?
5. What was Max's answer to William Hendred's proposal?
6. How far in the future was Max's St Mary's?
7. What triggered Max's flood of tears in Sick Bay?
8. Who was the elderly village priest in 14th Century St Mary's?
9. What did Max think was wrong with modern food?
10. What made Max think Walter had a sense of humour after all?
11. Who finally was able to make tea that Max could drink?
12. What was onion man's real name?
13. How long did Max have to stay isolated with no visitors?
14. How did Sir Hugh punish Max for setting fire to another of his properties?
15. How did Dr Stone know he'd never met Kalinda?
16. What had William Hendred been waiting for, before proposing to Max?
17. What did Max get accused of being in post-Waterloo Rushford?
18. How did William Hendred die?
19. What did Max find under the pod console?
20. What was Kal's shock therapy treatment?
21. Why did Clive Ronan shoot Dottle?
22. Who did Max end up agreeing to talk to?
23. What drove Max to clean Matthew's blue teddy?
24. What happened when Max tried to eavesdrop on Leon and Peterson?
25. When she hit the ground, what was Max thinking of?
26. Why didn't Max kick Dottle after pulling her to the ground?

Answers

1. Keep them in barrels of fresh water for a few weeks
2. Henry sent his personal, male, physicians to her and they had no knowledge of childbirth
3. Sir Luke the Jedi and the evil Dragon Darth Vader
4. None
5. She said she would tell him that night
6. 650 years or so
7. She thought she smelled Helen's cigarette smoke
8. Father Ranulph
9. Too salty, too rubbery, and too sweet
10. He sat Jerald in Lady Armstrong's chair
11. Mrs Partridge
12. Barden
13. Seven days
14. He made her owner of the useless yellow horse
15. He still had a full set of working testicles
16. For her to stop crying herself to sleep at night
17. A thieving jade
18. From an infected wound
19. An aerosol dispenser of a hallucinogenic drug called DMT
20. She pushed Max into the lake
21. She wasn't Annie
22. Dr Dowson and Professor Rapson
23. Mind-numbing boredom and desperation for something to do
24. She fell out of the window
25. Actium, sideways, and bracelets
26. Max wouldn't have stopped until she killed her

Notes

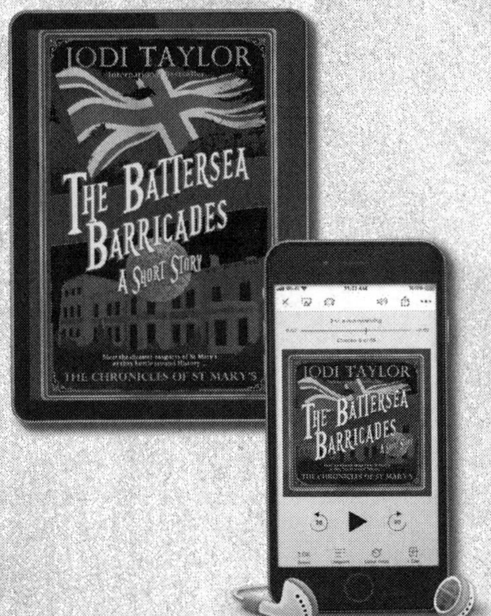

The Battersea Barricades

It's not easy being a rebel.

So many new skills to assimilate.

Never mind strategic planning, weapons expertise and the like - there's bicycle-stealing, oil-stain removal and boat-steering to be mastered first.

And quickly.

It's the time of the Civil Uprisings and two young women set out to make a difference.

Their only problem?

They don't know where they are.

Or where they're going.

Or what to do when they get there.

Other than that ...

Round One

Questions

1. If you start the fermentation process on St George's Day, when will your dandelion wine be ready to drink?
2. In a Constitutional Monarchy, what do wise politicians never do?
3. To where did the right-wing government despatch the old King?
4. Where did the Uprisings start?
5. Whom did Princess Mary marry?
6. Where in Cardiff did Princess Mary make her 'Enough is Enough' speech?
7. What was the traditional St George's day toast?
8. What luxuries did Mrs Enderby and Mrs Shaw enjoy?
9. What did the ladies make for the displaced homeless?
10. What had Theresa Mack's rebels done after Cardiff?
11. Why was Gloucester suddenly important?
12. How did the rebels disable the government force's scouts?
13. How long did the barricades at Gloucester last?
14. How did Mrs Enderby and Mrs Shaw try to get to London?
15. Where did the government forces stop the train?
16. How did the ladies find the Thames?

Answers

1. Midsummer's Day
2. Force the Monarch to say No
3. Scotland
4. Cardiff
5. A bearded palaeontologist
6. A derelict bookshop in West Bute Street
7. For those not here today
8. A roof, a bed, a locker, and two chairs
9. Tea and jam sandwiches
10. Disabled the Severn Bridges and blown up the tunnel
11. It was the lowest bridging point over the Severn
12. Home-made stingers to shred their tyres
13. Three or four hours
14. On the last train out of Gloucester
15. Reading
16. They pedalled round a corner and there it was

Round Two

Questions

1. What did Mrs Enderby describe as a dark and malevolent creature of evil that kept eating her coat?
2. How did Mrs Enderby persuade the boat to stop for them?
3. What sort of cargo was the narrowboat carrying?
4. What did the boat owner claim her cargo was?
5. What three ways can a narrowboat travel, according to Mrs Enderby?
6. Where did the River Police stop the boat?
7. What was the boat's return cargo?
8. How did the ladies know when they had reached their unplanned destination?
9. Which London landmark was the rebel's HQ?
10. What happened to Vauxhall Bridge?
11. How many Leviathans did the government send to destroy the rebels on Chelsea Bridge?
12. Who climbed onto the roof of a car and held up the Union Jack?
13. What did the rebels shout to the Leviathan pilots?
14. Who was the last person to die before the government withdrawal?
15. Who knocked on the door to summon Dr Bairstow?
16. What did Max suggest as the official definition of a Historian?

Answers

1. The bicycle she had stolen
2. She stuck out her thumb
3. Explosives
4. Textiles from Bolivia
5. Forwards, backwards, or straight down if you sink
6. Hampton Court
7. Injured people
8. A man came out of the fog with a rifle
9. Battersea Power Station
10. The rebels blew it up before the government forces could take it
11. Three
12. Mrs Shaw
13. "Enough is enough, stand down"
14. Trevor Mack, Theresa Mack's husband
15. Markham
16. Swilling wine and listening to stories of days gone by

Notes

The Steam Pump Jump

Not one to let being banged up in Sick Bay stop her, Max has had a brilliant idea. But she needs Markham to execute it on her behalf. The subject of this cunning plan is Peterson, struggling with his bereavement and not doing very well. What's needed to get him through it is sympathy, sensitivity, tact and understanding.

Step forward Mr Markham, for whom sympathy, sensitivity, etc., are things that happen to other people.

Combine a fanatic from R&D, a head of Security with his own problems, a steam-pump, two historians who can't even be in the same room as each other, some fractious Protestants and a large body of very dirty water.

Told in Markham's own words, this is the story of an intervention - St Mary's style.

Questions

1. Who was now the new Head of Security?
2. Why was Max in Sick Bay this time?
3. Why was Hunter worried about Family?
4. Who requested the Steam Pump Jump?
5. What was the 17th Century name for the Steam Pump?
6. Where was the jump to?
7. Who built the Steam Pump?
8. Who were the Deadly Duo that Evans was to keep an eye on?
9. What is Lingoss' first name?
10. Why were the Protestants visiting the castle?
11. What style beard had Markham grown and groomed for the jump?
12. What offended Markham about his costume?
13. What is the origin of the word "Cheerio"?
14. What were Sykes and North arguing about?
15. How did Lingoss end up in the moat?
16. What, as far as Lingoss was concerned, was the bright side of being in the moat?
17. What was Lord Herbert's only concern for people in the moat?
18. What was Lingoss' original hair colour?
19. Why did Lingoss originally dye her hair blue?
20. Why did Lingoss and Markham have to spend a couple of days in Sick Bay?

Answers

1. Markham
2. She had fallen off the roof
3. Markham had been warned not to have one
4. Lingoss
5. The Water Commanding Engine
6. Raglan Castle
7. Edward, Lord Herbert
8. North and Sykes
9. Felix. NOT Connie
10. To check for hidden Catholic weapons
11. A Van Dyck
12. It was pink (or rose)
13. "Chair Ho!" to summon a sedan chair
14. The Divine Right of the King
15. Markham pushed her
16. She got a close-up view of the steam pump
17. That bodies were not blocking the pump's water-intake valve
18. She couldn't remember
19. To prove her parents never noticed her
20. Immersion in, and ingestion of, foetid moat water

Notes

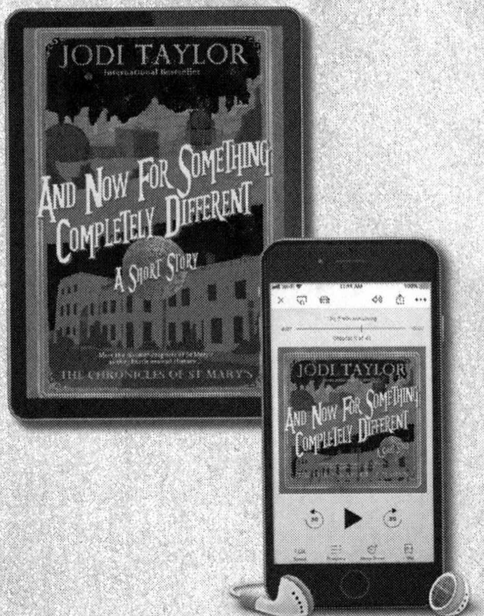

And Now For Something Completely Different

Every Christmas, for reasons which seem good at the time – especially after an eggnog or two – Max and the others leap into the nearest pod and indulge in their illegal Christmas jump. It's a tradition. This year, however, just to be different, they find themselves part of someone else's illegal Christmas jump. It's time to don a spacesuit and bring your own urine!

Questions

1. Which Pinkerton-era director of St Mary's betrayed them to Clive Ronan?
2. What was Pinkie's role before becoming director?
3. Where was the data stick hidden?
4. Whose unofficial job titles included Sacrificial Lamb, Buffer Zone, and Voice of Reason?
5. Why did Pinkerton feel her St Mary's had a duty to interfere on Mars?
6. Why did Pinkie take Max and Peterson to Mars to witness the first manned landing?
7. Why did Major Guthrie not accompany Pinkie to Mars?
8. Who was to judge the Build Your Own Spaceship competition?
9. What was unusual about Security Section's entry in the competition?
10. How did Pinkie's St Mary's solve the cosmic radiation problem?
11. What claim by Director Pinkerton did Commander Hay find particularly impossible to believe?
12. Why was Max unable to contribute to the radiation shield?
13. Where was the first manned Mars landing site?
14. What's Pinkie's definition of a good landing?
15. How much notice did the Martian landers get of the solar flare?
16. Why did First Officer Lewis not make it to the underground shelter?
17. What was a greater danger to Lewis than the solar flare?
18. Where did Pinkie take the unconscious Lewis?
19. Who did Pinkie take from Time Police Headquarters back to Mars?
20. What were Charlie's first impressions of Mars?
21. What did Max find on the rock wall of the lava tubes?
22. Why couldn't Max take Charlie's hand when she was starting to fall back into the lava tube?
23. Why did Hay say the St Mary's recording could never be released?
24. What phrase did Pinkie use that told Hay they had jumped off of Earth before?
25. Where had their previous space Jump been to?
26. What evidence of St Mary's presence did they accidentally leave on the previous space Jump?

Answers

1. Alexander Knox
2. Chief Technical Officer
3. In a fire bucket
4. Charlie Farenden
5. Because things didn't go wrong historically, so she had an obligation to make sure they didn't go wrong
6. To thank them for saving her St Mary's from Ronan
7. He was spending the day elsewhere
8. Pinkie
9. It was on fire
10. Urine-lined space suits and pod
11. That safety was their first priority
12. She had been to the loo before they left
13. Gale Crater
14. No bits fell off
15. 18 minutes
16. He had run into Pinkie's camouflaged pod and knocked himself out
17. Drowning in his own life-support suit
18. Back to her St Mary's
19. Charlie Farenden
20. Barren and unforgiving
21. A non-human hand print
22. She was holding her recorder
23. It would overshadow the 'real' first landing and end all space exploration
24. This time ...
25. Sea of Tranquillity, July 20th 1969
26. They caused the flag to flutter

Notes

Hope for the Best

Max is no stranger to taking matters into her own hands. Especially when she's had A Brilliant Idea. Yes, it will mean breaking a few rules, but - as Max always says - they're not her rules.

When History goes rogue, there's a St Mary's team right in the firing line and Max must step up.

You know what they say. Hope for the best. But plan for the worst.

Round One

Questions

1. Who was inspired by Max's sunflowers to try painting with pastels?
2. Where was Max going as part of her plan to deal with Clive Ronan?
3. What are Triple-Ss?
4. Who were the Albayans?
5. What problem was Matthew still having with his dirigible?
6. What contraband had Max tried to take with her?
7. What was new about Matthew on his visit from Time Police Headquarters?
8. What was Matthew's only stipulation about Friday Pizza Night?
9. How did Leon unsuccessfully try to lure Matthew away from R&D?
10. Where was the Time Police Headquarters pod bay?
11. Why did Max miss Dottle being cut from the tree?
12. Who did Max pair off with in her first Self Defence session?
13. Who did Max ask to cut Matthew's hair?
14. What shape was the Time Police Time Map?
15. Who went to see the new Star Wars film?
16. Who turned up with pizza after the Time Map incident?
17. When Max was trying regain weight, what was not allowed?
18. Who spotted the Time Map problem?
19. How did Max 'persuade' Matthew to have his hair cut?
20. What was wrong with London 1588?
21. Why did Max and Leon walk around the lake when they wanted to discuss important things?
22. How did Matthew cause chaos at Time Police Headquarters?
23. What did Lingoss want to ask Max?
24. Who did Max and the Time Police team need to keep away from London?

Answers

1. Matthew
2. Time Police Headquarters
3. Sites of Special Significance
4. The group within Time Police Headquarters who disapproved of Commander Hay and her changes
5. Steering
6. Tea bags
7. Flexiglove over his left arm to the shoulder and a plaster on his forehead
8. No anchovies
9. By telling him that, despite all the evidence to the contrary, they didn't blow things up every day
10. Under Battersea Power Station, and the Thames
11. She was in Sick Bay having her bones glued together
12. Grint
13. Lingoss
14. A three-storey high sphere
15. Matthew, Max, Leon, Peterson, and Lingoss
16. Ellis
17. Scarfing her way through plates of sausages and chocolate
18. Matthew
19. Expressly forbade him to ask Lingoss to do it
20. It was in a state of mass panic
21. Bad memories of having been bugged by Clive Ronan and Dottle
22. Breaking the Time Map
23. Did Max think there was hope for her and Peterson?
24. Mary

Round Two

Questions

1. What did the Time Police do to let the St Mary's team know where they were?
2. What was Max's theory about why they couldn't catch or kill Clive Ronan?
3. How did Max disguise herself at Hoddesdon?
4. What was, to her resentment, Max's physical fitness rating?
5. Who had been Queen for thirty-five years in the Tudor anomaly?
6. What absolutely vital technical component was conspicuous by its absence in the Time Police Pod Bay?
7. Where had St Mary's been evacuated to?
8. Where was the first Jump for which Max was to provide the historical background?
9. What single incident caused the Tudor anomaly?
10. What was the one thing Max admitted the Time Police do better and more smoothly than St Mary's?
11. Where were the coordinates Halcombe wanted Max to Jump to?
12. What did Max's contract with the Time Police say would happen if she were caught unescorted in the Map Room?
13. When Max returned to St Mary's from Tudor England, what was wrong?
14. How did Max gently disarm Grint?
15. Who got zapped by a Time Police sonic?
16. What was happening outside Tudor London that was causing the population to try to flee?
17. Who had taken over St Mary's?
18. What happened as the Time Police and St Mary's made their way back to the pod?
19. What colour did the world turn when Jumping in Mikey and Adrian's pod?
20. What caused London to start flooding?
21. What did Matthew paint?
22. What analogy did the Time Police use for Time?
23. What did Matthew say on seeing Mikey in Hawking?
24. Why was Max worried about St Mary's being in London on 19th August 1588?

Answers

1. Fired off a fizzer and caused a panic
2. He wasn't meant to die anywhere except in the Cretaceous
3. Wore the beekeeper's veil
4. A3
5. Lady Jane Grey
6. Duct tape
7. The remote site
8. Liverpool, 1826
9. Death of Bloody Mary
10. Landing a pod
11. Jerusalem AD33
12. They would shoot her
13. Everyone was gone
14. Hooked one leg behind his and kneed him in the face as he fell to the floor
15. Max
16. The Scots were marching South, the French had landed at Dover, and the Spanish were sailing up the River Severn and the Thames
17. Malcolm Halcombe
18. London Bridge exploded
19. Purple
20. The destroyed bridge dammed the river
21. The Time Map
22. A bluebell wood
23. "I'm going to marry her"
24. They should be at Tilbury recording Queen Elizabeth's speech

Round Three

Questions

1. Where did Max think Mary would go at Hoddesdon Manor?
2. What warranted cheering around Time Police Headquarters?
3. What did the private garden turn out to be?
4. Who did Max go to see after climbing down the chimney?
5. What happened to the two 'proper' Queens, Mary and Elizabeth?
6. What made the Teapot so special?
7. What did Max plan to do with the apples?
8. Who did Peterson ask Max to give his regards to?
9. What did Max see coming up behind them when running for the pod?
10. What was the establishment that Max needed to gain entry to?
11. How did Princess Mary react to Max's warning?
12. How did Max get into the detention centre?
13. Which additional hostage did Halcombe tell Sullivan to take on the Jump?
14. What did Max say that touched a nerve with Clive Ronan?
15. What did Halcombe threaten to do if Max refused to Jump to Jerusalem?
16. Who did Max bust out of Time Police prison?
17. What did Max remember Matthew had said about St Mary's?
18. What pushed Clive Ronan off Max?
19. What was the pod programmed to do after an illegal Triple-S Jump?
20. What was Demiyan Khalife's role?
21. Where was Max going to Jump to infiltrate St Mary's?
22. What almost drove Max over the edge into attacking Commander Hay?
23. Who did Max call on for help to infiltrate St Mary's?
24. What did Max find, when groping about in the mud?

Answers

1. Into the garden
2. They had 'caught' Adrian and Mikey
3. An orchard
4. Peterson
5. Summoned to London and murdered en route
6. It could remove things from their own timeline
7. Feed them to the bees
8. Lingoss
9. A white mist
10. A (very upmarket) sex club
11. Sent a letter to the Privy Council, and headed back to Norfolk
12. Told them Commander Hay had sent her?
13. Celia North
14. That he wanted to die
15. Throw her off the roof, repeatedly
16. Mikey & Adrian
17. "You've got good chimneys here"
18. A flash flood
19. Explode and kill everyone inside
20. Atticus Wolfe's personal assistant
21. Clive Ronan's hiding place on the roof
22. Being told she couldn't take Matthew home
23. Roberts and Sands
24. A snake-like creature

Round Four

Questions

1. Why did North come to see Max in Sick Bay?
2. Why couldn't Peterson give Max the coordinates of the remote site?
3. What do the St Mary's team and the clean-up crew need to make sure happens in 1554?
4. What did Adrian need to recharge the Teapot?
5. Where had people unwisely stood to get out of the rain during a fire drill?
6. Where was the remote site?
7. How did Max and Ellis distract Dudley's men?
8. What ranking did Max tell the bouncers that Atticus Wolfe was?
9. What did Max ask Captain Ellis to do with Matthew?
10. Who took over Directorship at the remote site when Dr Bairstow returned with Max?
11. Which Time Police Officer took care of Max's Jerusalem injuries?
12. What would be the biggest difference in a St Mary's version of Wolfe's club?
13. While running back to Hunsdon, what did Max trip over?
14. What did Markham say was the problem with changing keycodes and passwords every day?
15. What was the clue to the location of the alternate site coordinates?
16. What caused all the chaos at Kush?
17. Why shouldn't Ellis Jump back to Time Police Headquarters for reinforcements and more pods?
18. Where did Max Jump to, to fulfil Wolfe's demand for something unique and unfakeable?
19. Who was Leon bunking with at the remote site?
20. Why was it good for Max that Khalife shot one of the dodos?
21. What was Mrs De Winter's condition for helping Max?
22. What does Max give to Atticus Wolfe to prove she's gone renegade?
23. What were the others going to do while Max Jumped to the remote site?
24. What did Max suddenly realise was watching the nest when she stole an egg?

Answers

1. To find out if Max was dead yet, so she could apply for her job
2. He didn't know them
3. Thomas Wyatt's rebellion
4. A bog-standard caravan plug
5. Next to the oil tanks
6. Somewhere on the left-hand side of the landmass that would one day be known as North America
7. Faked a fight and kicked their lantern out
8. Fourth most powerful man in London
9. Leave teaching him to shave for Leon
10. Markham
11. Grint
12. Angus would be involved
13. A rabbit
14. People could never remember them, so wrote them down
15. 'Agincourt'
16. A snake
17. Every new Jump makes the timeline more fragile
18. Pinkie's St Mary's
19. Major Guthrie
20. It reminded her that the two men were dangerous, violent thugs
21. That she was to be involved in getting St Mary's back
22. Two dodos
23. Establish a base in the woods and reconnoitre St Mary's
24. A young Tyrannosaurus Rex

Round Five

Questions

1. What did North accidentally invent as a way to get information?
2. Where did Max suggest she take Wolfe to prove she could do as she claimed?
3. What had Lingoss put in Peterson's tea in Sick Bay?
4. What did Khalife shoot instead of the dinosaur?
5. What part of the pod did the white mist engulf?
6. Who happily stayed behind in Wolfe's club as a hostage?
7. About what did Mrs Partridge warn Max?
8. What happened when Khalife raised the price for Max?
9. When Max Jumped away from Jerusalem, how much time was left before the pod destroyed itself?
10. Where did Mikey Jump the Teapot to?
11. Where had Bashford given as his birthplace on a Thirsk University ethnicity form?
12. What did Khalife use to disable Max?
13. Where were the coordinates hidden?
14. Which cultural technology had the Kushites mastered, that the Egyptians had not?
15. What things would Max absolutely not advise investing in on pain of <redacted >
16. What feature, often required with pods, did the Teapot lack?
17. What was Professor Rapson attempting to make fuel from?
18. What did Wolfe decide they should bring back from the Cretaceous?
19. What was Max's perennial gripe with 'historical' TV and holos?
20. Why did Hay release Clive Ronan?
21. Why didn't Max want Sands to look around the future London?
22. Once they got back to Time Police Headquarters, what terrible news did Commander Hay give Max and Dr Bairstow?
23. Why couldn't Max and Ellis Jump to straight Hoddesdon?
24. What was SmartDust?

Answers

1. Waterboarding
2. Tutankhamen's funeral procession
3. Something that R&D had knocked up that tasted of whisky
4. Atticus Wolfe
5. One corner of the outer casing and the toilet
6. Adrian
7. Things that happened in her old world COULD happen in this one, but were not necessarily going to
8. Clive Ronan shot him
9. 45 seconds
10. The Kingdom of Kush, 720BC
11. Olympus Mons (lower left quadrant)
12. Her own stun gun
13. On the inside of the dust jacket of Max's Agincourt book
14. Horse riding
15. Zeppelins, canals, dirigibles, green roofs, intelligent glass, and energy generating walkways
16. Hydraulic legs
17. Livers (Probably not human, but ...)
18. A dinosaur egg
19. Women never had anything on their heads
20. Because he had not yet done all that they knew he would do
21. It would only depress him
22. Clive Ronan had already been released
23. Because after she left Hunsdon, they don't know where, Mary was poisoned in this bubble universe
24. A time bomb in Clive Ronan's brain

Round Six

Questions

1. What was Atticus Wolfe's educational background?
2. What did Wolfe suggest that Max bring him?
3. What had Max done surreptitiously before Sullivan attacked her?
4. What plan had Max decided on for dealing with Halcombe
5. Why did Mikey think being near to Time Police Headquarters was a good place to hide their pod?
6. What facial marker told Max that Wolf and Khalife probably grew up together?
7. What was Roberts not-very-demanding speciality at the University of Ceredigion?
8. Why did Leon say that Adrian and Mikey had to stay with St Mary's?
9. What were the names of the dodos Pinkie had crated up for Max?
10. Which God lived in the Inner Sanctum of the Jebel Barkal temple complex?
11. How did Max know she wasn't expected to Jump to Agincourt get the remote site coordinates?
12. What did Leon's beacon do?
13. How did Max know Wolfe had been expecting her?
14. What chaos did Khalife's gunshots cause at Kush?
15. What old password did Max give when challenged by Markham?
16. Even in the technical age, who is King (or Queen)?
17. What did Max blurt out accidentally on first meeting Wolfe?
18. How much did Adrian and Mikey bet on who would kill whom between Khalife and Wolfe?
19. Why was Lingoss wearing a beanie at the remote site?
20. What had the remaining dodo done while they were in Kush?
21. What did Wolfe ask Max to do before agreeing to anything?
22. Why had Dr Bairstow antagonised the Time Police enough to make sure they could never return to St Mary's?
23. How did Google say Max should treat her ganglion?
24. What choices did Max offer when the storm started up in the Cretaceous?

Answers

1. Marlborough and Sandhurst
2. Headed notepaper from the passenger lounge of the Titanic
3. Recorded what was happening outside of the pod
4. Pull his brain out through his nostrils with a crochet hook
5. Their signal would be swamped by all the Time Police pods' signals
6. The Kushite fold
7. The History of the European Union
8. "If you bring them home and give them a name, you have to keep them" (Like pets)
9. Hillary and Donald
10. Amun-Ra
11. Both she and Peterson had been at Agincourt in 1415 already
12. Transmitted a fake radiation signature that matched the one that the Time Police used to track the Teapot
13. Khalife called her Dr Maxwell
14. They spooked the animals
15. Horse's Arse
16. A clipboard wielder
17. "Have you ever had your portrait painted?"
18. A million pounds
19. Her hair colour was growing out
20. Laid an egg
21. Make a preliminary sketch
22. Because Leon had already rescued Matthew
23. Thump it with a Family Bible
24. Stay in the shelter of the trees, or return to the pod

Notes

A Storm in a Tea Cup

In which the catastrophes that befell St Mary's Christmas Day were absolutely not Max's fault in any way

Questions

1. Which storm caused all the trouble?
2. Who attached the concrete weights to the marquee to prevent it from blowing away?
3. How did Bashford attract the attention of the security services?
4. Why were so many of the Royal Family 'charging around the countryside' on Christmas Day?
5. Why did Bashford not put his hands on his head and surrender when instructed?
6. Who attacked and injured several members of the security services?
7. Around what did the marquee finally wrap itself

Answers

1. Storm Frances
2. No one
3. He was standing on the roof of his dead car with a chicken and a pair of binoculars
4. They were attending the 500th birthday of St Stephen's
5. He was unconscious
6. Angus, while defending Bashford
7. A bus (number 29)

Notes

When Did You Last See Your Father?

Have you ever wondered what would happen if Max's husband met Max's father? What would Leon do?

They're normally a fairly amiable bunch, but this is the story of what to expect if St Mary's doesn't like someone. As in, really doesn't like someone.

Warning: contains a unit-wide criminal enterprise, a great deal of illegal activity and a sad misuse of public resources. All the things a father will do to protect his family.

It is also a story of revenge. Because this is payback - St Mary's style.

Questions

1. What was Leon's mother's name?
2. What were the names of Leon's sons?
3. What killed Leon 's family?
4. Why couldn't Leon donate his own blood to save his sons?
5. Who found Leon drunk in a French bar?
6. How did St Mary's cure Leon's alcoholism?
7. What does Leon say to Max when he's tired of living?
8. Why do St Mary's always travel in pairs?
9. Who suggested peeing in John Maxwell's boot?
10. Where had the Historians been when they ruined Number Eight's toilet, broke both cupholders, acquired a dubious stain on one wall, and blew the secondary board all over the console?
11. What problem did Dr Bairstow come to see Leon about?
12. What was John Maxwell's job?
13. Who did Dr Bairstow say had pointed John Maxwell in the direction of Max and Matthew?
14. What did Leon say would happen if they kept the presence of her father a secret from Max?
15. What was Leon's plan B?
16. Which hospital did John Maxwell work at?
17. Why was it a mistake for John Maxwell to tell the police he'd been at St Mary's?
18. What huge mistake had John Maxwell made with Mrs Partridge?
19. What was Markham happy the police would find in the boot of John Maxwell's car?
20. What was Leon's plan C?
21. How did Max deal with her father's threats and insults?
22. Where did Mrs Partridge put R&D's concoction?
23. How did Mrs Partridge get John Maxwell's fingerprints on the hip flask?
24. Who 'enhanced' John Maxwell's laptop browser history?
25. Why did Dieter break John Maxwell's rear brake light?
26. Even if John Maxwell didn't go to prison, who would be very unsympathetic to his failure?

Answers

1. Grace
2. Alex and Stevie
3. The flu epidemic
4. He wasn't their father
5. Dr Bairstow
6. They gave him a drug that made him violently ill if he consumed alcohol
7. History isn't really that appealing
8. So there's always someone to bring back the body
9. Peterson
10. A genteel Edwardian tea party
11. Max's father had arrived
12. Surgeon-in-chief at a major hospital
13. Clive Ronan
14. Death and destruction of everything in a five-mile radius
15. A gun under his car seat
16. The Royal Free, Manchester
17. They hadn't forgotten having to get Bashford down from the church tower
18. Handing her his coat to hold
19. Carpet soaked in urine (very hard to explain)
20. Jump somewhere secret with Matthew
21. Said nothing and smiled at him
22. In the milk
23. Asked him to pick it up off the floor for her
24. Polly Perkins
25. He just wanted to be involved
26. Ronan

Notes

Why is Nothing Ever Simple?

It's Christmas at St Mary's and time for the traditional illicit jump.

Except this one is perfectly legal. It's Major Guthrie's last jump. To the Battle of Bannockburn, no less. An important moment in History for two nations - one that warrants everyone's full attention.

But Max soon finds herself grappling with a near-lethal game of pooh sticks, another avian incursion and two turbulent teenagers' intent on piloting their own illegal jump.

And that's all before they even get near fourteenth-century Scotland.

For this is St Mary's and nothing is ever simple . . .

Round One

Questions

1. Why did Major Guthrie decline a prosthetic eye?
2. What surcharge did Elspeth intend to levy on St Mary's personnel?
3. To whose account did more than one person charge their drinks at the St Mary's night out?
4. What advice had Max given the youngsters at a local school?
5. Why did Dr Bairstow not attend the night out?
6. Why did some of the St Mary's crowd find pooh sticks intellectually challenging?
7. Who fell into the river as human pooh sticks?
8. Why were people surprised when the human pooh sticks ended up in St Mary's lake?
9. What did Major Guthrie make for lunch with Max?
10. What did Major Guthrie need to talk to Max about?
11. Why was Markham not supposed to get anyone pregnant?
12. Why was Markham causing so much trouble when posted to Major Guthrie's unit?
13. What was Markham's final choice?
14. What accent did Markham have in the Army, and what did he change it to at St Mary's?
15. Where was Major Guthrie's final jump to be?
16. For which award would Max never be nominated?
17. Who nearly perished from the ever-expanding exothermic foam?

Answers

1. He wasn't Borg
2. Twenty percent
3. Max's
4. Always eat dessert first
5. It gave him plausible deniability
6. The were dropping the sticks downstream
7. Bashford and Keller
8. The river flows out of the lake
9. Chicken sandwiches and crisps
10. Markham
11. Because of who he was
12. To make it easier for Major Guthrie to get rid of him
13. Army or prison
14. Geordie to Bristolian
15. Bannockburn
16. Mother of the Year
17. Bashford

Round Two

Questions

1. What aroused Max's suspicions about Adrian and Mikey?
2. Which major safety protocol did Adrian and Mikey's pod not possess?
3. Who missed Major Guthrie's last jump?
4. Why did Adrian and Mikey feel it was their duty to make an illicit jump?
5. Where was the reception to be held?
6. Why couldn't Adrian and Mikey go to the party?
7. Why couldn't Elspeth Grey be a Historian any more?
8. What was a Schiltron?
9. Who went to Bannockburn with Max?
10. What did Robert the Bruce ride when facing up to Henry de Bohun on his huge warhorse?
11. What damage to the pod alarmed everyone?
12. What was the anomalous sniper wearing?
13. What information would it have been very useful to know before having a look at the captured sniper?
14. Who stunned Smallhope and Pennyroyal?
15. Why did Markham refuse to leave it to the Time Police sort out the assassins?
16. What was the name of the organisation the snipers belonged to?
17. Who offered Max and/or Markham a job?

Answers

1. They were talking quietly in a corner, in their 'battle dress'
2. The inability to jump back with contemporary objects onboard
3. Max
4. They had been invited, and it would be rude not to go!
5. Gonville and Caius College, Cambridge
6. Because they hadn't gone to the party (and it broke a bunch of rules)
7. She was 'pod-shy' - scared of time travel
8. A mass of men, linked together, with pikes bristling in all directions
9. Elspeth and Evans
10. A palfrey, a light riding horse
11. Bullet holes
12. A ghillie suit
13. Snipers work in pairs
14. Elspeth
15. Because they were a bunch of useless wazzocks
16. English National Liberation Army
17. Pennyroyal

Notes

PLAN FOR THE WORST

Max is quite accustomed to everything going wrong. She's St Mary's, after all. Disaster is her default state. But with her family reunited and a jump to Bronze Age Crete in the works, life is getting back to normal. Well, normal for St Mary's.

And then, following one fateful night at the Tower of London, everything Max thought she knew comes crashing down around her.

Too late for plans. The worst has happened. And who can Max trust now?

Round One

Questions

1. Who did Dr Bairstow suggest as Matthew's private tutor?
2. What project did Professor Penrose come up with to inspire Matthew to learn new skills?
3. Why couldn't Max sleep any more?
4. Where did Kalinda want to go to celebrate her return to St Mary's?
5. Who was Thirsk's replacement for Halcombe?
6. How did Professor Rapson intend to test his culturally appropriate safety headgear for the Crete mission?
7. Why couldn't Bashford go on the remote site FOD PLOD Jump?
8. What two crimes had Leon been accused of?
9. What was the main constituent of the new Microbial Fuel Cells to power the smoke alarms?
10. On what point did Max put her foot down and override Dr Bairstow?
11. What did Matthew warn Max?
12. What was Leon's wife's name?
13. Why was Celia North staying on with the Time Police?
14. What did Max threaten to do with Rosie Lee?
15. Why was Sykes given the latrine inspection job?
16. Why did Peterson and Markham tell Max to keep calm?
17. What did Mrs Partridge refuse to do for Markham?
18. How did Max get Rosie Lee out of her office?
19. What impressed the Vikings most?
20. What did Max find herself looking at when she was trying to get back to the pod?
21. What did the unknown person whisper in Max's ear?
22. What did almost everyone do after dinner with the Vikings?
23. What was the first thing the Vikings did to Max?
24. Who greeted the Viking chief open handed?

Answers

1. Professor Penrose
2. Building a robot PA for Markham
3. She was convinced that every sound was Clive Ronan or the Time Police sneaking into St Mary's
4. Crete
5. Kalinda Black
6. With a rapid chicken-firing gun
7. He'd fallen off his wardrobe
8. Murdering his wife, and then concealing himself in a time other than his own
9. Urine (according to Leon)
10. That she and Markham would accompany them
11. "You should stay away from the river"
12. Monique de Maupassant
13. There seemed to be a mutual attraction
14. Transfer her to Markham and the Security Section
15. She had been involved in the 'mammoth in the toilet' incident
16. The Time Police had arrived
17. Supply him with a PA
18. Asked her to wash up a dirty mug
19. Starting a fire in under ten seconds
20. A dragon
21. "Hello, little girl"
22. Play football
23. Feed her
24. Markham

Round Two

Questions

1. How many duvet days had Max had since her discharge from Sick Bay?
2. What did Ellis 'forget' to take with him?
3. What was on the hidden definitely-not-Time Police-standard data stick?
4. What alerted them to the fact that something was happening at the Tower?
5. How did Max surmise the Vikings got to the West Coast of North America?
6. What did they observe the princes doing at the Tower of London?
7. What did Markham want Max and Peterson to pose as?
8. What came out from the Watergate in the darkness?
9. What did Professor Rapson forget to do first when testing his chicken gun?
10. How could St Mary's prove the CCTV of Leon was faked?
11. Why was there no CCTV evidence of Leon leaving?
12. Why did Max decide to stay in the atrium at Time Police Headquarters and leave everything to Peterson and Markham
13. Who did Mrs Brown want to Jump to see?
14. What peculiar behaviour had Dr Bairstow noticed about the inhabitants of the Tower?
15. What went wrong with the Jump to the Tower of London from the start?
16. Why did Max go to see Commander Hay on her own?
17. Who was Mrs Brown?
18. What animal could be heard as they approached the Tower?
19. Why was Mrs Mack the most important person on the Crete assignment?
20. Why did Commander Hay personally walk Max back down to the atrium?
21. Where was the Big Jump planned to go to, taking almost everyone from St Mary's?
22. What did Max and Mrs Brown think that young Richard would be diagnosed with in more modern times?
23. Who interrupted the Crete briefing?
24. What did Markham go down with, according to Hunter?

Answers

1. Six
2. The Time Police file on Monique 's murder
3. CCTV of Leon going to Monique's apartment building on the night of her murder
4. One by one the torches and braziers inside the Tower were being extinguished
5. Through a melted Northwest Passage and Southwards from Alaska
6. Practice sword fighting
7. Auditors of Time Police procedures
8. A punt with three men in it
9. Defrost the chickens
10. The real Leon at that time was very ill and very thin. The Leon on the tape was neither
11. It was poor quality and never showed his face
12. She had 'history' with the Time Police that might prejudice their case
13. The Princes in the Tower
14. They ignored the princes, and three strangers walking around inside the walls
15. Pod landed outside the tower instead of inside
16. To apologise for her previous behaviour
17. Celia North's mother, Lady Blackbourne
18. A lion, roaring
19. She was going to be in charge of food
20. To make sure she didn't set fire to anything on the way out
21. Crete
22. ADHD
23. Matthew
24. Vomiting like Vesuvius

Round Three

Questions

1. What had Markham's robot PA done to him?
2. At Monique's apartment block, what did Max realise about one of the staff ID badges?
3. What disguise did Max adopt for Jumping to Mechelen?
4. What did Max spot in the crime scene photographs?
5. Who was trying to control the robot?
6. What stopped the three men from discovering the Team when watching the activity on the dock at the Tower of London?
7. What was Markham's breakfast special?
8. Why didn't Ellis recognise Isabella Barclay in the Time Police investigation?
9. Who turned the robot off?
10. What did the Team hear when making their way back to the pod?
11. What caused the great stench at Site B?
12. Why was Max an expert on pod rules?
13. Who crash landed Number Two into Hawking?
14. What did Max collide with while being dragged along the Thames by the current?
15. What went wrong with R&Ds experimental sun cream?
16. Who leapt into the Thames to save the child?
17. What sort of farm had Site B been set up near to?
18. Once inside the palace, where did Max head for?
19. What tree had been enclosed by a wall to make a shrine?
20. What was dragging Max under the water?
21. What special equipment had Kalinda persuaded Thirsk to supply for the Crete assignment?
22. In Max's hallucination, who was she married to?
23. What favour did Max ask Markham to do for her?
24. Who rescued Max from the Thames?

Answers

1. Poured boiling water into his groin area
2. Odette Duval's badge had Isabella Barclay's photograph
3. A nun
4. Travel tickets to England
5. Professor Penrose
6. They were called away by a fourth man
7. Grey dollops of porridge
8. He was not the investigating officer
9. Lingoss
10. A child's cry, and a splash
11. A dead badger accidentally thrown on the fire
12. She'd ignored or broken just about all of them at one time or another
13. Atherton and Prentiss, returning from an erupting Thera
14. An old jetty
15. It hardened to a shell, that turned out to be highly flammable
16. Mrs Brown
17. Bulls and cattle
18. The gardens
19. An oak tree
20. A broken piece of jetty, snagged in her dress
21. Seismology sensors for detecting earthquakes and eruptions
22. Len
23. Scare the living daylights out of Rosie Lee about the festering cup of tea
24. The Time Police

ROUND FOUR

Questions

1. How much longer was Hunter's pregnancy?
2. What was the unenviable claim to fame of William, Lord Hastings?
3. What happened just after Max saw Clive Ronan?
4. What had really happened when Max thought she had Jumped to Burgundy?
5. What animal was sacrificed to start the proceedings?
6. What was Max's biggest concern should anything happen to Mrs Brown?
7. What unexpected consequence of the earthquake had Max, Peterson, and Markham running for their lives?
8. Who was the little boy in the Thames?
9. Who did Clive Ronan shoot on Crete?
10. How did Dr Bairstow betray Max?
11. What separated Max and Peterson when escaping the Cretan earthquake?
12. Why did Dr Bairstow have to save Markham not Max?
13. What did Max think had caused Clive Ronan's death at first?
14. Who was tied to the tree in the shrine?
15. What did Clive Ronan want?
16. Who did Max's Dr Bairstow nominate as his successor if he died?
17. Where did Clive Ronan intend to Jump to?
18. How did Max disable the priestess?
19. Who found Max exhausted in Wardrobe?
20. What was the name of Hunter and Markham's baby?
21. What did Dr Bairstow say had happened?
22. What was the dark line on the horizon that set off all the St Mary's pod alarms?
23. What was happening in Knossos while St Mary's were there?
24. What was Markham's thank-you gift to Max?

Answers

1. Just over two weeks
2. The first person to be executed within the walls of the Tower of London
3. A small earthquake
4. Mrs Partridge had drugged her, and she had slept while false memories and the warning were implanted
5. A white calf
6. That Celia North would hunt her down
7. The bulls were loose
8. Richard of York, and also Markham
9. Peterson
10. He rescued the boy, not her
11. A landslip
12. Because Markham lived to be an adult, in his future, and to let him drown would have brought disaster to everyone
13. The SmartDust
14. Markham
15. Mikey and Adrian's Teapot
16. Peterson
17. The moment of Annie's death
18. Stuck a couple of hairpins into her arm
19. Markham
20. Flora
21. That there had been an accident and Max fell in the river
22. The giant tsunami
23. Preparations for a big public festival
24. To be baby Flora's first visitor

Round Five

Questions

1. What did Max surmise made the high priestess appear to glow?
2. What did Max finally decide had caused Clive Ronan's death?
3. What did Max give the future Dr Bairstow?
4. What did Max think caused the famous Minoan women's chest- and buttock-protruding stance in Cretan paintings and frescoes?
5. How many bull jumpers were there?
6. Whose bullet killed Annie Bessant?
7. Why did Max say the Teapot was dead?
8. Why was Max so furious with Dr Bairstow?
9. In Minoan royal culture, who took precedence and left the stands first?
10. What year did Thera erupt?
11. What was the only thing in Knossos that had survived?
12. Where did Dr Bairstow take the boy?
13. Who brought the Teapot to Crete?
14. What did the bull-masked man with the axe do in the arena?
15. What did Markham claim his first name was?
16. What did Max find out from the servant boy?
17. After the Jump, what was wrong with Clive Ronan's eyes?
18. What geological anomaly did Max think Crete had?
19. What was Markham's letter about?
20. What was the A word that no one wanted to say in connection with Thera or Crete?
21. How did Clive Ronan finally die?
22. How did Max interrupt Clive Ronan's explanation of his plan?
23. What was the Labrys?
24. What did Max think was better than running away from her problems?

Answers

1. She had been dusted with powdered gold
2. He had Jumped too close to where he already was in time
3. The coordinates of the Cretan hillside
4. Their tight, wide, metal belts
5. Seven - five girls, two boys
6. Clive Ronan's
7. So that it and Clive Ronan would be swept away and destroyed by the water
8. He'd interfered with history, and left one of his people behind
9. The High Priestess
10. 1628BC
11. The bull's horns above the city
12. To his aunt, the Duchess of Burgundy
13. Dr Bairstow
14. Killed the mortally wounded bull Jumper
15. Markham
16. That Dr Bairstow had delivered the prince just after dawn
17. One pupil had swollen to cover the whole iris, one had shrunk to a pinprick
18. Everywhere was always uphill
19. Warning him not to have children
20. Atlantis
21. His convulsions broke his spine
22. Kneed him in the balls
23. The Minoan doubled-headed axe
24. Staying put and kicking the living shit out of them

Notes

The Ordeal of The Haunted Room

What could be better for the annual festive jump than the chance to experience a real Victorian Christmas?

On the longest night of 1895, a terrible storm rages above Harewood Hall. Max, Markham and an injured Peterson are welcomed in by the Harewood family, but soon realise that, in true St Mary's style, they couldn't have arrived at a better moment. For tonight marks the Ordeal of the Haunted Room. Dum ... dum ... dum ...

Every Harewood heir must endure one terrifying night alone in the Haunted Room before he can inherit the family seat. Legend says that a ghost will murder anyone who isn't the true successor.

Henry Harewood's ordeal will begin at midnight and end at dawn, but it isn't long before everything goes horribly wrong...

Round One

Questions

1. Whose fault was everything?
2. Who was Barnstaple?
3. Who introduced Christmas trees to the UK in 1800?
4. What were the Harewoods' first names?
5. How did even medically-untrained Max know that Peterson's foot was not looking good?
6. What were the footmen's names?
7. What was Mrs Trent's role in the Harewood household?
8. According to legend, what happened to the young usurper of the Harewood Hall estate when the rightful heir returned?
9. What job did Millie have?
10. What would happen to anyone not the rightful heir during the night of the Ordeal?
11. Who was the first to document the phrase "Dead as a doornail"?
12. What was the baby's name?
13. If the current Mr Harewood did not survive the Ordeal, what would happen?
14. What was the name of the Harewoods' family solicitors?
15. What was the Reverend's name?
16. What did Max claim her husband was studying?

Answers

1. Max's fault
2. The Harewood's butler
3. Queen Charlotte of Mecklenburg-Strelitz
4. Henry and Letitia
5. Feet should not be spherical
6. John and Thomas
7. Housekeeper
8. Locked in a room until morning, and committed suicide in the night
9. Parlourmaid
10. The ghost of the usurper would kill him
11. Shakespeare
12. Jamie
13. The estate would be kept in trust until his son reached 21
14. Chance, Venture, Chance, and Spigot
15. Lilywhite
16. The Moche culture in Peru

Round Two

Questions

1. Why did the reverend criticise the Winter Solstice?
2. Which maid helped Max with her hair for dinner?
3. Whose hands scuttled over the table like white spiders?
4. How many locks were on the door of the Haunted room?
5. Who took the keys from Chance and Lilywhite and unlocked the door?
6. Who broke down the remaining lock?
7. How did Max get fresh air into the Haunted Room?
8. Where did Mrs Harewood suspect the poison had been?
9. Which book had Mr Harewood taken in to the Haunted Room to read?
10. What roused Mr Harewood from his stupor in the Room?
11. What did Mr Harewood senior write on one of the paper spills before he died?
12. How did Barnstaple prevent the murderer's escape?
13. Why did Chance need to kill Mr Harewood?
14. Which gas did Chance use to kill Mr Harewood Senior, and almost kill the present Mr Harewood?
15. Which was the only breakfast item that Max ignored?
16. Who was Mrs Harewood's great-great-multiple-greats granddaughter?

Answers

1. It was a pagan celebration
2. Eliza
3. Reverend Lilywhite's
4. Three
5. Max
6. Barnstaple and John
7. Smashed the window panes with a walking stick
8. In the decanter
9. The Iliad
10. A burn on his arm
11. The name of his murderer
12. Grabbed his coat tails and knocked him unconscious
13. To prevent him reading the estate accounts, and funding out that Chance had been stealing from it for years
14. Carbon monoxide
15. The porridge
16. The pilot of the Leviathan that refused to open fire on the Battersea Barricades

Notes

Another Time, Another Place

It's long been known that if a thing can go wrong, it will. With knobs on, usually. Disasters start to pile up. A new colleague with no respect for the past and a great deal to prove. Historians lost in time. And - worst of all - Rosie Lee on her very first jump. Then there's the small matter of Max's dishonourable discharge.

From Tudor England to the Tower of Babel - it's all going horribly wrong.

Jobless and homeless, Max receives an offer she can't refuse. Another time, another place. A refuge, perhaps. She's got that wrong, too.

Round One

Questions

1. Where does Angus the chicken like to sleep?
2. Who was going with Leon in TB2?
3. What did Max tell Dr Bairstow his real job was?
4. What was Leon's new mission?
5. Who did Dr Bairstow appoint as acting Head of Security in Markham's absence?
6. Whose death was Max going to take Hyssop to witness?
7. What enticing options did Max offer Leon?
8. Where did Dr Bairstow want Max to take Hyssop?
9. Who was had Hyssop been, before being seconded to St Mary's?
10. Why was Treadwell's opinion more important than Peterson's?
11. What was Captain Hyssop's new role at St Mary's?
12. Why did Hyssop say she was reluctant to grow her hair?
13. How did Hyssop offend Max?
14. Who had vanished at the same time as Dr Bairstow?
15. What was Hyssop's second responsibility?
16. What did Max lecture schoolchildren on?
17. What was the nickname given to Captain Hyssop's new security personnel?
18. What was the first thing Treadwell raised with Max?
19. Name the Halfwits
20. How did Dr Bairstow die?
21. What was Peterson's Option B regarding Hyssop?
22. Who intervened in Max and Treadwell's row to calm things down?
23. Where did Peterson want Max to visit with him?
24. Why did Dr Dowson keep a hard hat on his desk?
25. Who was stretched out on the floor of the History department?
26. What was the main reason that Max and Hyssop didn't clash during the first half of the Babylon mission?

Answers

1. On top of Bashford's wardrobe
2. Adrian, Mikey, and Matthew, plus Professor Penrose
3. To make the right decisions, not the nice ones
4. To find a suitable new Remote Site
5. Evans
6. Amy Robsart's
7. Full-on, head-banging sex or a bacon butty
8. On a Jump to somewhere non-lethal
9. The Army
10. He was the new director of St Mary's
11. Temporary Head of Security
12. It frizzed up in a giant ball when long, which might frighten the horses
13. Calling her 'Miss' Maxwell
14. Mr Strong
15. Health and Safety
16. Riots, revolutions, battlefields, bloody murders, executions, torture, plagues, pus...
17. Hyssop's Halfwits
18. Angus
19. Scarfe, Lucca, Glass, Harper, Jessop, and the other one whose name no one can ever remember
20. Car accident on the way to London
21. Murder her and bury the body in the sunken garden
22. Peterson
23. The church
24. His locker is on the opposite side of the building
25. Bashford
26. They were in separate pods, a quarter of a mile apart

Round Two

Questions

1. Who was stretched out on the floor of R&D?
2. What made Max almost fall in the same way as Amy had?
3. What had happened to Prentiss and Clerk?
4. Where was Amy Robsart staying?
5. What colour tiles was the city of Babylon famous for?
6. Who grabbed Max's skirt and saved her from falling?
7. Who barred the Halfwits from the Dining Room?
8. Why did Mrs Oddingsells not want to go to the fair on Sunday?
9. What classic St Mary's diversion did Max use to enable them to rescue Clerk?
10. Who did not feature in Treadwell's briefings by his employers?
11. Who was waiting for Max in her room at the Falconburg Arms?
12. Who was having afternoon tea with Dr Bairstow on the terrace?
13. What else were Matthew and Professor Penrose taking with them when they went with Leon?
14. What did the Halfwits try to bring on the assignment?
15. Who did the Historians assume was the man who came to the house?
16. Who were the only people on Hyssop's list of personnel for the Babylon Jump?
17. Why did the experiment to see which hand people would automatically use to defend themselves fail?
18. What food was given away at the festival?
19. What did Mrs Oddingsells and Mrs Owens do instead of attending the fair?
20. Why was Max unhappy with Hyssop's team allocations?
21. Who tried and failed to take charge of the Robsart Jump?
22. Why did Peterson think Treadwell wanted a more Security personnel than Historians?
23. What was the fatal staircase made of?
24. What was the first Max knew of the problem in Babylon?
25. What were the four possibilities put forward for Amy's death?
26. How many Jumps would Treadwell allow to find Clerk and Prentiss?

Answers

1. Bashford, again
2. The newel post was covered in polish
3. They had been arrested by the temple guards
4. Cumnor Place
5. Blue
6. Hyssop
7. Mrs Mack
8. That was the day for the commoners to attend
9. Set something on fire
10. The Time Police
11. Pennyroyal
12. Mrs Brown
13. R2-Tea2
14. Blasters
15. Sir Richard Verney
16. Herself and her halfwits
17. Bashford had no survival instincts (he once waved to Boudicca)
18. Flatbread with goat and mutton
19. Played cards in their rooms
20. There were no experienced Security personnel with the Historians
21. Hyssop
22. To replace Historians with Security personnel on Jumps
23. Stone
24. Hyssop turned up, alone and unannounced
25. Accident, killed by an unknown lover, killed by her husband's man, or killed on the orders of the Queen
26. Only two more

ROUND THREE

Questions

1. Who made the decision to enter the courtyard of the temple?
2. What gaps had been in Treadwell's files about Mrs Mack, Mrs Enderby, and Mrs Shaw?
3. What had Hyssop forgotten to bring on the mission?
4. Who was Kevin Aguta?
5. What was on offer for Max after her dismissal?
6. Why was Glass' inclusion on the Babylon Jump at risk?
7. Where did Max and Sands get a tag reading?
8. What showed that Amy was expecting an important visitor?
9. Who kept Markham informed about things at St Mary's?
10. What did Max note would be useful for future assignments to hot desert towns?
11. Where had Clerk seen Prentiss?
12. Who remembered to wipe the polish from Amy's hand?
13. Who were Max and Markham going to pick up in Victorian London?
14. Who surprised Max by knowing how to pilot a pod?
15. What did Max notice about her dismissal paperwork?
16. Who did the time police deliver to St Mary's?
17. What did Markham want to call the pair of them?
18. How did Max intend to ignore Treadwell's limit on rescue Jumps?
19. Why could Max and Markham take no weapons with them on their pick-up job?
20. Where did Scarfe sneak into?
21. What event did both Max and Markham badly want to attend?
22. Who insisted on Jumping back with Max to rescue Clerk and Prentiss?
23. What news did Smallhope bring that stunned Max and Markham?
24. What did Max threaten to do to Scarfe?
25. What was Dr Bairstow's biggest fear for the Archive?
26. How did they distract the merchant's nephew long enough for Prentiss to slip away?

Answers

1. Hyssop
2. Their crucial roles in the Uprisings and the Battersea Barricades
3. Tag readers
4. The vicar of St Mary's parish
5. A job as a bounty hunter - sorry, Recovery Agent
6. He didn't seem to be able to grow a beard
7. At the brickworks
8. A grand chair, a silver wine goblet, and honey biscuits
9. Ian Guthrie, via Pennyroyal
10. Fly whisks
11. Fetching water from the river
12. Hyssop
13. Winterman and Feeney
14. Evans
15. It had all been prepared well in advance of her dismissal
16. Halcombe and Sullivan after their thirty-year sentences
17. Pros and Cons
18. Set up a relay of Historians, Jumping two there, two back indefinitely, so it would be classified as a single Jump
19. The Time Police made hefty deductions for damage to the merchandise
20. The inner sanctum
21. Peterson and Lingoss' wedding
22. Rosie Lee
23. Dr Bairstow was not dead
24. Leave him in Babylon
25. The government taking it away and censoring, altering or even destroying it
26. Rosie Lee flirted with him

Round Four

Questions

1. What was the problem with bringing Clerk and Prentiss back from Babylon?
2. Where was Dr Bairstow being held?
3. What did Clerk do to find out which building Prentiss was in?
4. Where did Max wake up from her nightmare?
5. What method was Max going to use to gain access to the house in Swan Court?
6. What reason did Max give the Red House staff for transferring Dr Bairstow?
7. Why did Markham warn Max not to turn round?
8. What did Gaunt do to Max?
9. What did Feeney offer Max?
10. What did Prentiss name her baby?
11. Who opened the door to number 6, Swan Court?
12. Based upon Max's (possibly unreliable) dating, what year was current in her St Mary's?
13. Who was in charge of the Swan Court household?
14. What was Sands' ongoing joke about who he worked for?
15. Who was Peterson's best man in the absence of Markham?
16. Why might Queen Elizabeth have wanted to rule Dudley out as a suitor?
17. What was Martin Gaunt's role at the Red House?
18. What was the final conclusion about Amy Robsart's death – murder or accident?
19. How did Lingoss arrive at the church?
20. What is the first golden rule of conflict negotiation, according to Max?
21. What position did Sullivan put Max in?
22. What did Max mentally add to her bucket list?
23. What had happened to Mrs Brown?
24. How did Max identify Queen Elizabeth?
25. What did Halcombe say he was going to do after he killed Max?
26. Where did Max visit the replica of the Ishtar Gate when she was an archaeologist?

Answers

1. Prentiss was pregnant
2. At the Red House
3. Sang behind them in English, until he heard one with a baby crying
4. Handcuffed to a bed in the Red House
5. Posing as a collector of charitable subscriptions
6. Treadwell had screwed up
7. She looked better from the back
8. Cut off her hair
9. Tea
10. Max
11. Jack Feeney
12. 2050 or thereabouts
13. Mrs Proudie, the cook
14. That he worked for Cunard
15. Sands
16. She had more freedom and power as an unmarried woman
17. Head of Security
18. Impossible to say
19. Driving a carriage pulled by Turk
20. Shoot the bastards before they even start to argue
21. Strappado - kneeling, with her arms forced straight back and up
22. Find Alexander the Great's tomb
23. Under house arrest
24. By the Chequers Ring she wore
25. Get Matthew
26. Berlin, the Pergamon Museum

Round Five

Questions

1. Why did Max warn the staff at Swan Court not to touch the banknotes or the sovereigns?
2. What did Professor Rapson think he could make batteries out of?
3. How did Max get Feeney to lean close enough to throw the Teapot at him?
4. How did Max realise that Treadwell had been very thorough in his background checks of St Mary's staff?
5. When had a mysterious 'someone' hired Smallhope and Pennyroyal to locate and rescue Dr Bairstow and Mrs Brown?
6. What new feature did Peterson ask Max's opinion on?
7. Who shot whom in the Red House?
8. What did Max hope would happen to Hyssop while in Babylon?
9. What was Markham's Plan B?
10. How did Treadwell react to the rescue relay?
11. What organisation did Treadwell work for?
12. Where had Max decided to leave Clerk and Prentiss?
13. Who supplied the genuine transfer documents for Dr Bairstow?
14. What trade was Prentiss's owner?
15. How did Markham open the handcuffs?
16. What excuse did Max give Sands for warning him, all those years ago, not to drive into Rushford?
17. What happened when Markham tried to hypnotise a chicken?
18. How did Max get Prentiss out of the shop?
19. Who was waiting for Max in her bedroom at the farm?
20. According to Max, who runs the world while the politicians think they do?
21. Why had everybody gone to so much effort to ensure St Mary's personnel were safely dispersed through time?
22. What was the name of the family who worked the farm?
23. Who did Markham give a good kicking to upstairs in Swan Court?
24. What did Max say she was collecting donations for in Victorian London?
25. Who was the silk merchant's nephew?
26. What was in the centre of Swan Court?

Answers

1. Sooner or later enquiries would be made, and any sign of pilfering would be punished
2. Lemon juice and copper rods
3. Pretended to read the tea leaves
4. He knew how she liked her tea
5. Before their supposed accident
6. His new glasses - which actually did make him look both intelligent and sexy
7. Hyssop shot Halcombe and Sullivan
8. That she'd fall into the Euphrates and get eaten by a hippo
9. Throw Max out of the window
10. Ended all searching except one more, two-person Jump
11. The Time Police
12. Patara, on the Ionian coast
13. Mr Black
14. Silk and cloth merchant
15. He bent one of Max's hair clips and picked the lock
16. She'd had a dream where he crashed
17. He got badly pecked, then the chicken's friend turned up and he got pecked again
18. Pretended to faint so needed a female slave to help her
19. Dr Bairstow
20. The administrators
21. Because the Time Wars were starting
22. Faraday
23. Josiah Winterson
24. The Rotherhithe Seamen's Mission
25. Abilsin
26. A plane tree

Notes

THE TOAST OF TIME

It's that most wonderful time of the year once more. But Max and Markham are a long way from St Mary's. What sort of Christmas will it be without their loved ones?

Settle down with a mince pie and a small sherry and prepare for an unlikely combination of Flying Auctions, Fabergé eggs, duped Time Police officers, the Parish Council, a TWOCed Bentley (no, not that one), legendary swords and a belligerent ram.

Will it be Peace and Goodwill to all men? Well, we all know the answer to that…

Questions

1. What kills 99% of all known germs on dropped toast?
2. Where were Max and Markham living away from St Mary's?
3. What job were they doing now?
4. What was their new assignment?
5. Where was the flying auction to be held?
6. What were the only specific instructions Pennyroyal gave Max and Markham?
7. Where was Amelia when Max and Markham went to the auction?
8. Whose perfectly genuine credit card did Max take with her?
9. What was Markham's fun fact about rams?
10. What was the newest building in 1920s Rushford?
11. What was Markham's suggested team name?
12. What was Max's preferred team name?
13. Whose sarcophagus was at the Auction?
14. Where was the panel from the Amber Room from originally?
15. What was the incredibly ugly cup?
16. Which Michelangelo painting was on display?
17. Which sword was at the auction?
18. What was the back page rule in the auction catalogue?
19. Why did the auction end abruptly?
20. Who volunteered to be searched first?
21. What is Max's go-to procedure in times of crisis?
22. What interrupted the searching of the customers?
23. What did Markham manage to steal?
24. What's the St Mary's difference between a discussion and a brisk discussion?
25. How did Max smuggle herself into St Mary's?
26. How did Max unwisely determine if Vortigern was dead?
27. How did Max disguise herself in the kitchen?
28. Who was the only person who recognised Max?
29. What high tech equipment does a librarian need to crack open modern security cases?
30. What world event coincided with the Parish Council meeting?
31. Whose car did Markham hotwire?
32. Where did Max and Markham hide their loot?

Answers

1. Marmalade
2. Home Farm
3. Bounty Hunters (or Recovery Agents)
4. To attend a flying auction
5. St Mary's Priory 1921
6. Don't get caught
7. Christmas shopping in Harrods
8. Smallhope's
9. If a ram backs away from you, he's just increasing the length of his run-up when he charges
10. A petrol garage
11. Pros and Cons
12. Literally anything else
13. Menkaure
14. The Catherine Palace, near St Petersburg
15. The Jules Rimet Trophy
16. Leda and the Swan
17. Durendal, the sword of Roland the Paladin
18. No one was allowed to leave until the auction was over
19. One of the exhibits had been stolen
20. Max
21. Set the place on fire
22. An explosion outside
23. Two Fabergé eggs and Durendal
24. Brisk discussions involve bloodshed
25. Helping the bread man
26. She poked him
27. By making toast
28. Peterson
29. A bent paperclip
30. Naked Gardening Day
31. Mrs Huntley-Palmer's
32. In Ian Guthrie's secret cellar

Notes

A CATALOGUE OF CATASTROPHE

Punching well above their weight, Max and Markham set out to bring down a sinister organisation founded in the future - with a suspicious focus on the past.

Max's focus is staying alive long enough to reunite with Leon and Matthew, alternately helped and hindered by St Mary's. Who aren't always the blessing they like to think they are.

But non-stop leaping around the timeline - from witnessing Magna Carta to disturbing a certain young man with a penchant for gunpowder - is beginning to take its toll. Is Max going mad? Or are the ghosts of the past finally catching up with her?

Round One

Questions

1. How did the attackers enter the farmhouse?
2. Who had been dismissed from St Mary's?
3. What did Pennyroyal leave on Max's bedside table at Home Farm?
4. Where did Max propose hiding Dr Bairstow and Mrs Brown?
5. What did Max's attacker hiss in her ear?
6. Who, was it decided, would Jump to future London and reconnoitre?
7. What did Max kick back out of the door?
8. How was Markham able to narrow down the search for the real villains to being Insight?
9. They are not Bounty hunters. What are they?
10. Why would Max and Markham need accommodation?
11. What did the logo on the torn piece of paper look like to Max?
12. Where had Max seen Bridget Lafferty before?
13. Who are Max & Markham working with/for?
14. What sort of job was Max going to apply for, and why?
15. What happened while Max was waiting in the pod for Markham's return?
16. When Bridget got a call during the interview, what did Max recognise
17. How did Max kill Bridget?
18. What name did Max adopt to infiltrate Insight?
19. How did Max write the coordinates down with no pen?
20. Where did the black file have a map of?
21. Where did the coordinates Max had obtained from the attackers' pod lead to?
22. Who cut Max's Gaunt-ravaged hair?
23. Where had the attackers' pod Jumped to?
24. Who definitely did not wear a toupee?

Answers

1. Through the roof
2. Evans
3. Night visor, blaster, handgun, and stun gun
4. Swan Court, Victorian London
5. "You bitch - I could have loved you"
6. Markham
7. Two gas canisters
8. Their logo matched the 'ice cream cone' scrap of paper
9. Recovery Agents
10. They couldn't live long term in a pod, and Markham couldn't live at all with Max's snoring
11. A hand holding an ice-cream cone
12. In the attack on Home Farm, where she had died
13. Smallhope & Pennyroyal
14. Admin, because admin staff can legitimately go anywhere
15. The autopilot engaged and Jumped away
16. The code she wrote down was the one on the scrap of paper
17. Fell down the stairs with and on top of her
18. Maxine Forrest
19. She cut her arm and used her blood
20. The Thames, near Windsor
21. Future London
22. Markham
23. A warehouse
24. Eddie Middleditch

Round Two

Questions

1. How did Max know she would get the job?
2. What was the magic word to open the attackers' pod?
3. Where did the coordinates Max wrote on her thigh refer to?
4. What was peculiar about the Home Farm attackers?
5. Which floor was Max not allowed on at Insight?
6. What did Max see, just as she was about to Jump back to Home Farm?
7. Who did Max follow after the fake Time Police broadcast?
8. What identity was it decided Dr Bairstow and Mrs Brown should adopt at Swan Court?
9. What colour were the files in the locked cage?
10. Where did Max go while the builders were repairing Home Farm?
11. What was Max's plan to ensure the letter got to Lord Monteagle?
12. Why shouldn't Max lay down a trail of breadcrumbs to avoid getting lost?
13. Where did Max write the Jump coordinates?
14. Who came to see Max minutes after she arrived in the Falconburg Arms?
15. Who was the only person who could forge the letter to Lord Monteagle?
16. Who did Max hear over her com at Runnymede?
17. Who did Max encounter under the House of Lords?
18. Who did Treadwell warn Max to avoid?
19. Where did Markham take Max after the Gunpowder Plot?
20. What was Max's Brilliant Idea to flush out Insight at Runnymede?
21. Why couldn't they find the pod outside the House of Lords?
22. Who went back to Home Farm with Max?
23. Where did Max, Leon, and Matthew go?
24. What, apart from the Time Crimes, was the biggest difference between St Mary's and Insight?

Answers

1. How else would she have known Bridget Lafferty
2. "Please"
3. Runnymede, 1215. The Magna Carta
4. They were wet and slightly charred
5. The top
6. A torn piece of paper on the floor
7. Bridget
8. Mr and Mrs North
9. Black
10. To see Leon
11. They write and deliver it themselves
12. They attracted mice
13. On her thigh
14. Treadwell
15. Dr Dowson
16. Someone from Insight
17. Guido Fawkes
18. Martin Gaunt
19. Swan Court
20. Peterson, Sands, and Roberts would impersonate the Time Police over the com
21. Max had activated the camo device
22. Evans
23. A cottage in Streetley, near Rushford
24. Insight would leave their people behind

Round Three

Questions

1. Once back in London, who came knocking on the door of Swan Court?
2. What logo was stencilled on the stationery cupboard at Insight?
3. Where did Max think the next assassination attempt would take place?
4. Where was the rendezvous point for both Home Farm teams?
5. What did Max realise the two goons were there to do?
6. How did Markham introduce himself to Bridget?
7. Where was Max taken to during the siege at Lincoln?
8. How did Max and Markham fool the guards in Jacobean London?
9. Why was Pennyroyal concerned about the miscreants' injuries?
10. What did Max realise Eddie's real job was?
11. What excuse did Max give to leave Lady Nicola and go back down to Markham?
12. How did Max get out of the cottage?
13. Who dealt with Rat Face and Smuggy?
14. Who did Max walk into at Runnymede?
15. What was Max's disguise at Lincoln Castle?
16. How could Max tell she wasn't a princess?
17. What specific job did Max apply for?
18. Where was Bridget's 'tertiary location'?
19. How did Max disrupt the assassination of Lady Nicola?
20. How did Nurse Fortunata disguise Max?
21. Where did they land the pod in future London?
22. Who had come to kill Max at the cottage?
23. When did the attack on Lincoln Castle start?
24. Who arrived at St Mary's Sick Bay to arrest Max?

Answers

1. Rat Face and Smuggy - miscreants!
2. Skull and Crossbones
3. Inside Lincoln Castle
4. London, the House of Lords, 1605
5. Kill Winterman and Feeney, and install new 'paying tenants'
6. Mark Ham
7. The top of the Observatory Tower to meet Lady Nicola de la Haye
8. He pretended to be drunk and singing, while she berated him
9. The Time Police paid less for damaged goods
10. Security
11. That she could aid the wounded
12. Through the bathroom window, onto the outside toilet roof
13. Evans and Dr Bairstow
14. Peterson
15. Hander-out of pasties
16. She always had to rescue herself
17. Filing clerk
18. The Battle of Lincoln, 1217
19. She told the snipers to go to the secondary site to kill William Marshall
20. Shaved off her hair, and covered her with dressings and bandages
21. In the block of flats' garden
22. Bridget and Insight
23. After breakfast and prayers
24. Martin Gaunt

Round Four

Questions

1. How did Max explain her haircut to Bridget?
2. How did Markham get Max back from her hallucinations?
3. How long had Max been gone in the attackers' pod?
4. How did Sykes attack the sniper?
5. Who was the assassins' real target at Runnymede?
6. Why did Markham have to leave?
7. Who did Hyssop work for?
8. What could you have done with King John's nose?
9. Who was left to interrogate the attackers at Home Farm?
10. What plan precipitated Max's disastrous morning at the cottage?
11. What does the acronym SPERM stand for?
12. Once they had time, what problem with their pod did Max and Markham need to address?
13. What was Pennyroyal's secret to tasty pasties?
14. What did Professor Rapson's small diversion primarily consist of?
15. Why did Leon say it was a good thing Treadwell only allowed Hyssop's halfwits to go on assignments?
16. What was the strong chemical smell that Max recognised from the warehouse?
17. Who did Max contact at St Mary's after coming down the chimney?
18. How many days early did Max and Markham arrive?
19. Who was Max fixated upon being the villains in Future London?
20. How did Max refer to Professional Historians?
21. Who did Peterson enlist to create a 'small diversion' while Max talked to Dr Dowson?
22. Where did Lord Monteagle live?
23. What was Bridget the first boss ever to say to Max?
24. How many assassins did they capture at Runnymede?

Answers

1. A short-sighted flatmate with blunt scissors
2. Slapped her, hard, twice
3. Three days
4. She bit him
5. William Marshall
6. To keep Hunter and Flora safe
7. No one knew - possibly not even Hyssop
8. Used it to slice cheese
9. Pennyroyal
10. Making soup
11. Society for the Preservation of English Regalia and Monuments
12. It was starting to drift
13. Get them from Greggs
14. Flesh-eating beetles
15. If someone were to attack St Mary's, only the real Security Section would be there to defend it
16. Fire retardant
17. Peterson
18. Ten days
19. The British Museum
20. Pains in the arses, all of them
21. Professor Rapson
22. Hoxton
23. "You're making me look really good"
24. Four

Round Five

Questions

1. What big mistake had Max and Markham made about Insight's plans?
2. After the soup failure, what did Max try to cook next?
3. Who, did it turn out, had employed Smallhope and Pennyroyal to locate and rescue Dr Bairstow and Mrs Brown, should it ever be necessary?
4. What caused the commotion on the North wall of Lincoln Castle?
5. How do the Time Police deal with the problem of 'Time Drift'?
6. What did Leon do for lunch after Max's cookery attempts?
7. What had Insight's pod been programmed to do if no safety code was entered?
8. Where did the soldiers drag Markham to get the pot off his foot?
9. Who did Markham attempt to give the forged letter to?
10. What did Max shoot at the Insight team?
11. What happened to Mrs Proudie's house keys?
12. What did Max work out was the crucial point that Insight could disrupt?
13. What was plan A at the House of Lords?
14. Who came to see Max in Sick Bay, and was surprisingly civil?
15. Who were incorporated into Insight?
16. What nightmare returned to Max after they landed in London?
17. What was Max initially unable to see in the undercroft?
18. Why was taking Max through the Great Hall Martin Gaunt's big mistake?
19. How did the British Museum respond when Insight beat them to something?
20. What did Max find Markham doing in the Jacobean tavern?
21. Where were Insight on 4th November 1605?
22. Who else turned up to arrest Max?
23. What did Max work out was the aim of Insight's interferences?
24. What was causing Max's disorientation and hallucinations?

Answers

1. Assuming they were working chronologically
2. Cheese on toast
3. Dr Bairstow
4. William Marshall's relief force had been sighted
5. They spend some time with the Time Map to ground themselves
6. Took them both to the pub
7. Shut down life support, close the door, then self-destruct
8. To the drunken blacksmith
9. Lord Monteagle's servant, Thomas Ward
10. Three fizzers
11. Max gave them back to Mrs Proudie, who gave them to Mrs Brown, who gave them back to Mrs Proudie
12. Monteagle warning Cecil and showing him the letter
13. Markham went into the undercroft, lugged out a barrel of gunpowder, and raised the alarm
14. Hyssop
15. SPOHB, SPERM, and the Historical Ships Records
16. The Ripper monster
17. The gunpowder
18. Hyssop was there, and arrested her for Treadwell's murder
19. A frigid memo in a dead language usually
20. Conjuring tricks
21. Waiting to intercept the letter at Hoxton
22. The Time Police
23. That the English Parliament never happened
24. She was starting to drift, like an overused pod

Round Six

Questions

1. What cool new hobby had Matthew taken up?
2. What did the remote in the woodshed operate?
3. What was the connection between the letter to Lord Monteagle in the National Archives, and the one Dr Dowson wrote?
4. Who did Markham remind Max about when arguing they needed to be the ones to save Parliament?
5. Where did Matthew say 'something' was?
6. What was the sentence from the toe-curling confiscated book that Max's English teacher had used to teach basic grammar?
7. Which printers did Markham get his parchment, ink, and quills from?
8. What was Max's plan if she'd died after the attack at the cottage and woke up in Heaven?
9. What did Mrs Brown offer?
10. Where did Max actually wake up?
11. How did Markham convince the servant to take the letter?
12. What had Leon installed, upstairs and down, disguised as thermostats?
13. After some months at the cottage, what old hobby did Max restart?
14. Who had been sent to guard the cottage until Leon could get there?
15. Why did History not deal with the assassins at Runnymede?
16. What was Sands' latest book about?
17. What was worrying Matthew?
18. Who saw Treadwell being shot?
19. Who sallied out to meet William Marshall?
20. What worried Leon about Matthew finding out that Max was massively under triple arrest?
21. What had persuaded Leon that the cottage was the place for them?
22. How did Max signal to Peterson that the Time Police were, in fact, Markham, Ian Guthrie, and Evans?
23. Why couldn't Max and Markham return to Home Farm for food, water, clean clothes, and recharging the pod, so had to stay in London for ten days?
24. What name did Hyssop arrest Max under?

Answers

1. Trainspotting
2. R2-Tea2
3. They were the same letter; Dr Dowson 'forged' the original
4. Aline
5. In the woodshed
6. "Algernon, take me, take me, my body is on fire for you"
7. Christopher Barker, at the sign of the Tyger
8. Get herself expelled before lunch
9. To find somewhere safe in Max's own time for her to recover
10. St Mary's Sick Bay
11. Told him that if he didn't, he would not survive the next day
12. Panic buttons
13. Painting
14. Glass
15. Because History had already arranged things so that Max, Markham, and St Mary's would be there
16. Three species of humans vying in a millennia long battle to wipe each other out
17. Fear of messing up his exams
18. Max and Hyssop
19. Geoffrey de Serlant
20. That he wouldn't be shocked
21. The silver birch woodland at the back
22. By using the code phrase Horse's Arse
23. Because any Jump might be Max's last
24. Lucy Maxwell

Notes

The Good, The Bad and The History

St Mary's is under investigation. Their director has been shot and Max is Number One Suspect. Can things get any worse? We all know the answer to that one.

Then there's the small matter of Insight - the sinister organisation from the future hell bent on changing History for their own dark ends. Having successfully infiltrated their ranks, Max is perfectly placed to stop them. But she knows her cover will soon be blown - because it's already happened.

Can Max take down Insight before they come after her? The circle is closing, and only one can survive…

Round One

Questions

1. How was Bashford and Roberts' return from a nocturnal excursion disrupted?
2. Where did Max go after her time in Sick Bay was up?
3. What book did Max unexpectedly discover in the Egypt - Middle Kingdom section of the Library?
4. Who was trapped in the fire by the loom in the doorway?
5. When the police came to interview Max, what alias did she give?
6. Where was Matthew going to do his sixth form studies?
7. Who was left behind to care for Pennyroyal?
8. Who finally shifted the loom?
9. What did Max tell the police caused her the facial injuries?
10. How had Pennyroyal booby-trapped the safe?
11. What name did Pennyroyal mutter in his fever delirium?
12. How many volumes did Max and Markham rescue?
13. Who could Max well believe was an ancestor of Commander Hay?
14. What statues guarded every entrance to the academy buildings?
15. Why were the Chinese anti-foreigner rebels called Boxers?
16. Where were the encyclopaedia volumes kept?
17. Who did Max, in her fake librarian persona, dump in the mire over the shooting of Treadwell?
18. How did the librarians try to save the books from the fire?
19. Where would the teams take the rescued volumes?
20. What was "talking-in"?
21. What was the Yong-le Dadian?
22. Why did Max need time before returning to work at Insight?
23. After searching through piles of books rescued by others, what did Markham and Max reluctantly decide they had to do?
24. Why did Bridget want to see Max on the Monday?

Answers

25. Angry swans
26. The Library
27. A book on Chinese History
28. A woman and her daughters
29. Nicola Hay, Librarian
30. Time Police Headquarters
31. Max
32. Evans and Markham
33. An airbag in a car collision
34. With an acid bomb, to destroy the contents - and the safe-breaker's face
35. Derek
36. Four each
37. Lady Nicola de la Haye, Constable of Lincoln Castle
38. Open mouthed dragons
39. From their name The Righteous and Harmonious Fists, and their fighting rituals
40. In the Han Lin Academy
41. Lucy Maxwell
42. Threw them in the lotus ponds
43. Back to St Mary's for them to sort out their discovery
44. Reorientation after being away from somewhen for a long time
45. An eleven thousand volume Chinese encyclopedia from the early 15th Century
46. For her hair to grow back and her bruises to fade
47. Rescue the encyclopaedia volumes themselves
48. To suggest she apply for an Insight internal competition

Round Two

Questions

1. Whose portrait of their founder did Insight have on the wall of the top floor?
2. When Max went to look for Markham at the Academy, what happened to her?
3. What would Max's role in the 'other' Insight be?
4. Where did Markham find Max in the burning academy?
5. Who was Geoff?
6. Why didn't the Chinese soldiers shoot Max?
7. How did Max allay all Geoff's worries that he'd said too much?
8. What profession had Clerk taken up in Patara?
9. What was Max's tactic to rattle Geoff?
10. When she ran away from the execution site, what did Max fall into?
11. What did Max do after completing the first stage of her training?
12. What happened the day after handing in her report, as Max arrived at work?
13. How did Max gain maximum enjoyment from her session in the firing range?
14. Where did Max and Markham go for a rest?
15. How would Max have known where they had landed even with her eyes shut?
16. What was Max 's prize for winning the essay competition?
17. What did Geoff reveal was Insight's real business?
18. What did Max have to do for the competition?
19. What plans did Max secretly nurture for Geoff?
20. What did Bridget begin by offering Max?
21. What did Max actually do to Geoff?
22. Even though her speciality was Ancient History, why wouldn't Max choose to live there?
23. What unique office accomplishment had Rosie Lee managed?
24. Where was the secret side of Insight?

Answers

1. Clive Ronan
2. She was caught, recognised as a looter, and dragged before a firing squad
3. Teach clients about their selected time, and accompany them for a couple of weeks to help them familiarise themselves
4. Back at the execution site
5. Max's unpleasant new mentor at Insight
6. They were called away to defend the walls by an officer
7. Max asked if she could go into Insight's bright new future world with him
8. Baker
9. Interrupt him and ask so many questions he would never get to finish a sentence
10. The open sewer
11. Return to her filing clerk job, and have her photograph taken receiving her prize
12. Bridget took her upstairs to the Boardroom
13. Imagined Geoff spread-eagled on the target
14. Patara, to see Prentiss and Clerk
15. The uniquely old smell of the Valley of the Kings
16. A gift certificate, and an unspecified 'something extra' from Bridget
17. Changing history
18. Research and write up a piece on where in History she would live if she could
19. Bash him on the head with a rock and push him off a cliff
20. The chance to travel as part of her job
21. Pretended to pull him out of the way of a rockfall, but 'accidentally' pushed him off a cliff
22. Slavery, famine, disease, warfare, bad-tempered gods, no medicine and dentistry, no hot water, no women's rights, and no chocolate
23. She'd killed her artificial plant
24. In the second-hand bookshop next door

Round Three

Questions

1. Why did Bridget want Max to enter - and win?
2. How did Max stop Eddie and the others just shooting all the Egyptians and looting the donkeys?
3. Why did Bridget want to see Max next day after Egypt?
4. What did Kleio say caused the devastation?
5. What was Max's plan while Eddie was delivering files throughout the building?
6. What did Eddie make Max do at the Egyptian tomb?
7. What did Bridget ask Max to consider?
8. What was the name of the little boy playing in the park?
9. What did Bridget do that completely blind-sided Max?
10. What was in the donkey panniers?
11. Why was Bridget going to accompany Max on her first real assignment?
12. What was Max's choice?
13. Which era and place did Max write her report on?
14. Who did they almost leave behind in Ancient Egypt?
15. What was Max's first assignment?
16. Why was Mrs Partridge always proud of Max?
17. How did Max nearly give the game away to Bridget?
18. What came up behind Max in the Valley of the Kings?
19. Who had to get back inside Insight, and disable their pods?
20. What would have happened if she'd let the little boy die?
21. Where was the Insight pod bay?
22. Why was the lost donkey more important than the others?
23. What had happened to London while Max was sitting outside Time Police Headquarters?
24. Who suggested Anastasia's new name to her?

Answers

1. To rub their professional historian noses in it by being outdone by a filing clerk
2. Warned him of the loose rock and the avalanche risk
3. To invite her to lunch and congratulate her on upsetting Geoff
4. Max chose wrongly
5. To rootle through his desk
6. Get the first donkey
7. An easy, friendly, relationship with her
8. Clive Ronan
9. Invited her out for a drink
10. Nothing
11. She liked her company, and Geoff refused to ever go in a pod with her again
12. To stop him being run down by the bus or not
13. 1920s England, and Rushford in particular
14. Geoff
15. A resettlement
16. She always did the Right thing
17. Mentioned tea and biscuits
18. A hyena
19. Max
20. Someone who Clive Ronan would have killed would destroy the world
21. Behind the door in Bridget's office
22. His panniers were still full of treasures
23. It had been replaced with vast piles of blackened rubble, and a river of bones
24. Helen Foster's ghost

Round Four

Questions

1. Who was Derek?
2. What special role did Bridget have in mind for Max?
3. Why was Markham doing the hoovering in just a pinny?
4. Why did Anastasia want pizza?
5. What excuse did Max give for not wanting intimate relationships?
6. Where had Smallhope hidden Anastasia?
7. What coded message did Markham pass on to Max?
8. How did Max get a message to Markham.?
9. Where was the client to be resettled to?
10. Where did Max and Anastasia hide while trying to escape?
11. What did Bridget offer after hearing about Max's childhood trauma?
12. What did the Time Police mech give Max?
13. What was Max's first task for the new assignment?
14. Where did the Emergency Extraction Jump to?
15. What steps had Svetlana taken to ensure she left no traces at Insight?
16. How did Markham cause chaos inside the Insight building?
17. Where did Bridget take Max for lunch after telling her what would happen to the clients?
18. Why was no one at St Mary's when Max Jumped there from London?
19. Where did Max take Anastasia for an ice cream?
20. Who was down in the pod bay?
21. Who led Insight's team of murderers?
22. Who did Max hold at gunpoint in burning Rome?
23. What exhibit fascinated Anastasia?
24. How did Dr Bairstow intend to respond to the threat of government control?

Answers

1. The last surviving member of the squad responsible for Pennyroyal's sister's death
2. Part of an assassination team - planning, briefing, organising, and putting Eddie in the right place to take the shot
3. To make sure Bridget left the flat as quickly as possible
4. She'd never had it before
5. Her rape by her father at age nine
6. In the silver room, with the key inside
7. Smallhope and Pennyroyal would be in the flat in one week
8. Wrote it on a napkin, used it to wipe pizza from Anastasia's face, and dropped on the bench for him to pick up
9. Swan Court
10. In the pantry
11. To arrange her father's death, or to dig up his corpse and jump on the bones
12. A com set disguised as a disc player, six EMPs disguised as discs, and a door lock disabler
13. Prepare a briefing document for Svetlana and Anastasia
14. St Mary's, on the lawn
15. Refused all food and drink, kept her hands in her lap, and wore plastic fingertips
16. Locked all the fire doors, then set off the fire alarms
17. The British Museum private dining room
18. Big all-hands mission to the Great Fire of Rome
19. The British Museum
20. Bridget and her hit squad
21. Eddie
22. Ellis
23. The winged, human headed lions
24. By moving St Mary's completely out of the UK

Round Five

Questions

1. Where were most of the professional librarians?
2. Who turned up just in time to prevent Max being shot by the Time Police?
3. Who were Hitler's Little Helpers?
4. After the MP's threats had been dealt with, who burst into the meeting?
5. What was Ian Guthrie's usual welcome for St Mary's staff?
6. How did Max persuade Ellis to bring his teams to deal with Insight?
7. What was the safe word between Max and Markham's if someone else was present?
8. Who took charge of the meeting in Dr Bairstow's office?
9. What was Clerk and Prentiss' third child's real name?
10. What gifts did Markham give Dr Bairstow?
11. What additional anti-infiltration method did Insight use to protect their pod bay?
12. Who had Insight put in St Mary's as their inside man?
13. Who had given Clerk and Prentiss enough gold to buy out the old baker?
14. What was Evans' big decision he needed Max's advice for?
15. What name did Max give the donkey?
16. Who was next to burst in to the meeting?
17. What activity did Max and Markham join in at the Pear Tree pub?
18. Who did Max have to see before leaving St Mary's?
19. Who stole the gold from the other donkeys' panniers?
20. What was Treadwell's warning Jack Daniels and Martin Gaunt?
21. What did Bridget say would happen to Max if she said No?
22. What was the government's plan?
23. What less-well-publicised services did Insight offer selected members of staff?
24. What 'new' role did Dr Bairstow offer Max after everything had calmed down?

Answers

1. The Annual Cataloguers' Conference Cataloguers' Cataloguing Competition (in Criccieth)
2. Hyssop
3. The Time Police's anti-assassination section
4. Martin Gaunt
5. "Oh god, go away!"
6. Told him he could wrap up the entire organisation, and be promoted to Major
7. Orchid
8. Markham
9. Marietta
10. The sword of Durendal, two Fabergé eggs, and two yellow silk-bound volumes of the Yong-le encyclopaedia
11. A dark, long, loud, metal spiral staircase
12. Dr Stone
13. Treadwell
14. Whether to go off with Smallhope and Pennyroyal or stay at St Mary's
15. Ramses, because his nose reminded her of Ramses II
16. Smallhope and Pennyroyal
17. The pub quiz night
18. Jack Daniels
19. Smallhope and Pennyroyal
20. That there were now death warrants for both of them if they ever breathed a word of the day's events
21. A simple injection of a selective mindwipe drug, then wake up next morning with no memory of the day
22. To put St Mary's under their direct control
23. Sexual services
24. Chief Operations Officer

Round Six

Questions

1. What was Max pretty sure would actually happen if she said No to Bridget's job offer?
2. What name did Pennyroyal use while posing as the butler?
3. How did Insight control pod console access?
4. Who turned up in the sixth pod?
5. What was the password for getting through the front desk of the fake bookshop?
6. Who was Mrs Danvers really?
7. Who did Insight intend to assassinate?
8. Where did Max send Pennyroyal?
9. Where did Max decide to live while undercover at Insight?
10. How did Max blackmail Treadwell into supporting her over Anastasia?
11. What would be the consequences of the assassinations and other interferences Bridget intended?
12. Who came out to offer (unwanted) assistance to the Time Police as they took Insight's building apart?
13. What did Max admit to Bridget when they got back from Egypt?
14. What had been Clive Ronan's main purpose of the whole 'I want to stop running' charade?
15. What was Bridget's ultimate goal?
16. What did Treadwell admit?
17. Why did Max want to release the donkey in Russell Square Gardens?
18. Who shot Dr Stone?
19. How long, according to Markham, do all mammals take to pee?
20. What was Dr Bairstow's concern about the anti-drift medication from Treadwell?
21. Where did she tell Markham they had to take the donkey?
22. Who adopted Anastasia?
23. How did Max plead for help from Mrs Partridge?
24. Who was the new, seriously scary, head of Medical?

Answers

1. An 'accident', killing her and Markham
2. Jeeves
3. Each person had a personal code to unlock and relock the console
4. Eddie and Pennyroyal
5. "The folio edition"
6. Smallhope
7. George Washington's grandfather
8. Back to Home Farm
9. In her trainee flat above the bookshop
10. Mentioned she'd met all three children at Patara
11. To keep America under the British Crown
12. Sarah Greenwood, of the Provisional Wing of the British Museum
13. She only brought the donkey back to piss off Geoff
14. To kill Helen Foster and insert Dr Stone
15. To be running Insight
16. That for years he had helped someone live out of her own time, moving her around, until she was an adult
17. Because she could secretly meet with Markham
18. Commander Treadwell
19. Twenty seconds
20. That Dr Stone had substituted a very different set of pills
21. To St Mary's via Home Farm
22. Peterson and Lingoss, under the name Helen Peterson
23. She claimed Sanctuary
24. Dr Rosemary Salt

Notes

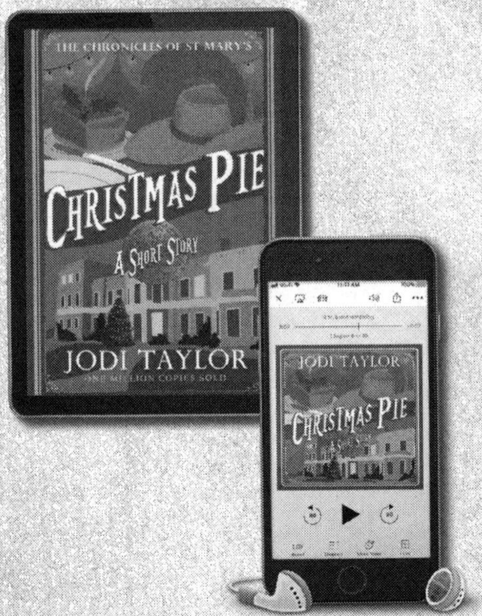

CHRISTMAS PIE

St Mary's has never lacked for enemies, but danger has never been closer to home. A state of war has broken out between St Mary's and the Raffia Mafia.

Markham, Max, Peterson and Miss Sykes must Jump in search of real Christmas pie - the honour of St Mary's is at stake.

At least that how it all begins, but this is St Mary's after all...

Round One

Questions

1. What must the reader consume each time they spot one of Markham's puns?
2. Where does Angus spend most of her days?
3. Who were the Raffia Mafia?
4. Where did Markham suggest Jumping to get an authentic Christmas Pie and recipe?
5. What was Sykes' new role?
6. Which ensemble made its return for Markham's costume?
7. What did Max think should be a banned substance?
8. Who gave Sykes her ultimatum?
9. How did Markham try to find Sykes?
10. Who had taken Sykes prisoner?
11. What was important, opposite St Swithin's church?
12. Who was the tall blond goon?
13. What had everyone forgotten after Bannockburn?
14. Who was the Benedictine monk?
15. Why did Markham think he was the one who had been hit on the head?
16. What was Angus' nest made of?
17. What was Sykes' cunning plan to bring pies back out of their own time?
18. What happened to anyone consuming contemporary foods while on an assignment, once they returned to St Mary's?
19. Why didn't Mrs Mack accompany the others on the Jump?
20. By what name was tea referred to in Restoration London?

Answers

1. A mince pie
2. In the stables
3. The Women's Institute
4. Restoration London, December 1661
5. Head of Training
6. The rose suit and feathered hat
7. Milk
8. Roberts
9. He stood on a chopping block, and shouted her name
10. The English National Liberation Army
11. The London Stone
12. Kester di Maggio
13. ENLA teams work in pairs
14. Markham's brother, King Edward V
15. There was no Bashford to fill the 'concussed' role
16. Bashford's old cricket jumper
17. To announce loudly that they would eat them later, thus marking them for destruction which would enable them to be taken back to St Mary's
18. Extra time in Sick Bay
19. She's not that stupid
20. The Indian Drink

Round Two

Questions

1. Why did Sykes need the midden again?
2. Which piece of equipment chose the worst time to work?
3. Why would Sykes go off with unknown random people?
4. What crunched under Markham's foot?
5. Which stupid myth did ENLA believe?
6. What did Markham tell the goons his job was?
7. Who disabled two ENLA goons with a wooden alms tray?
8. What had changed about Roberts when he came back to St Mary's from Wales?
9. With six mince pies each for twelve tables, how many pies did Max say there were?
10. What did mince pies of the Restoration period look more like?
11. Why were there no signs with prices?
12. What bit of the Sword in the Stone legend do people always forget?
13. How did Markham know that two of the goons were amateurs?
14. What had Hunter made very clear to Markham?
15. Why was the 'Walter Raleigh throwing a cloak over a puddle' both a myth and a reality?
16. Who did Markham tell about the need for the pie recipe?
17. How did Hunter demonstrate she knew Markham better than anyone?
18. What book arrived on Dr Bairstow's desk the day after the Jump?
19. What metaphor fell upon Markham when talking to Sykes about her dilemma?
20. Who sliced the London Stone in half?

Answers

1. The cold - and the company
2. The tag reader
3. Because she's Sykes
4. Sykes' earpiece and com
5. "He who controls the London Stone controls England"
6. Admin
7. North
8. Taller, well built, bearded, handsome, more Welsh
9. 74
10. Pork pies or small bread loaves
11. Everyone local knew how much a pie was
12. The anvil
13. Top-turned boots, fur trimmed cloaks, and no hats
14. Handcuffs are only acceptable in certain social situations
15. Everyone there except the woman who turned out not to be the Queen was a time traveller
16. Pennyroyal
17. She knew he wanted another child, a boy he would call Edward
18. "The English Huswife" by Gervase Markham
19. The Anvil of Enlightenment
20. Markham

Notes

LIGHTS! CAMERA! MAYHEM!

Coming to a screen near you...

TEMPORA, THE TIME TRAVELLING TOURIST

Starring Astrid Gustafsson as Helen of Troy - 'the face that launched a thousand ships' (Homer)

With Dirk Thrust as Achilles - 'demi god and hero' (Homer)

And the Wooden Horse as Himself - 'easily the least wooden performance from anyone participating in this particular travesty' (Dr Maxwell)

Watch and weep as this epic tale unfolds...

Round One

Questions

1. Who really runs Cavendish Cutter Productions?
2. What sort of 'Um…' did Adrian approach Max with?
3. Where did most people, plus R&D, the pods and the Archive, go while Calvin Cutter and his team were at St Mary's?
4. Why was Peterson hanging out of Max's window?
5. Who had been assigned to escort Astrid around St Mary's?
6. What was wrong with Calvin Cutter's thoughts on the sets for Troy?
7. What did Astrid hate most about her role as Tempora?
8. What was Max's biggest surprise on meeting Astrid?
9. What awards did Astrid and Joan of Arc win?
10. How did Max's trained eye spot that Adrian was besotted with Astrid?
11. Why did Evans find Astrid so attractive?
12. What had Adrian done that was monumentally stupid?
13. What attacked Adrian's drone at Troy?
14. Why did Adrian have to exit the pod at Troy?
15. Why were tag readers pointless?
16. Where did they find Astrid?
17. Who had Astrid been mistaken for in Troy?
18. Where did Mrs Enderby say she was from?
19. What was the first deviation from History (and common sense) in Calvin Cutter's Troy?
20. Who was to fight Achilles instead of Hector?
21. What were Calvin Cutter's Greeks going to make the Wooden Horse out of?
22. What did Max plan for the scriptwriters of Tempora one day - and Calvin Cutter as well?

Answers

1. Marj
2. The sort that precedes an apocalypse
3. The remote site
4. His office faced the wrong direction
5. Max
6. He believed Troy looked the same as Egypt, plus ziggurats
7. The skintight silver outfit that restricted her ability to eat, drink, or even wee
8. That she was very nice and impossible to dislike
9. The BADs - Book Adaptation Disaster awards
10. He wore clean T-shirts and combed his hair
11. She was the first woman he'd ever met who was his size
12. He'd taken Astrid to Troy and lost her
13. An eagle
14. He couldn't leave the anomalous drone there
15. Astrid wasn't tagged
16. At a ceremony in the Temple of Athena
17. The goddess Athena
18. Welwyn Garden City
19. Helen would be dead
20. Tempora the Time Travelling Tourist
21. They disassembled their own ships
22. A quick one-way trip to the Cretaceous

Round Two

Questions

1. Where did the money come from to fund the BADs?
2. What was the rule on female footwear for the BADs awards?
3. How many nipples were on show at the previous year's BADs?
4. Why was Astrid's clever speech accepting her BADs award wasted?
5. How did Peterson explain the appeal of Tempora for Adrian to Max?
6. What was forcing Mrs Enderby to be terribly brave?
7. How did Max suggest the wicked Pharaoh could die?
8. What had been the general impression of Astrid before people met her?
9. Whose idea was it to take Astrid to Troy to let her see for herself what it was like?
10. What disrupted the ceremony at the Temple of Athena?
11. Who did Max, Markham, and Evans encounter on their way to the Temple of Athena that evening?
12. What disrupted the escape back to the pod?
13. Who now had a classroom permanently at St Mary's?
14. Who else turned out to be surprisingly good fun and likeable?
15. What did Adrian tell Astrid Leon's pod was?
16. Why was Max the best person for Adrian to come to when he'd done something stupid?
17. What happened to Adrian when he tried to retrieve the drone?
18. Who was the keeper of the database showing who was when and where during the Troy assignments?
19. What would be the quickest, if most shameful, solution to the disaster?
20. Why hadn't Evans been in Troy on the vital day?
21. Why did Max and Markham have to be away from Troy before midnight?
22. How did Max distract the eagle from Evans and Markham?

Answers

1. The slighted author's royalties for the unmitigated disaster that was the adaption of his work
2. If you can walk properly in your footwear then you're not allowed in
3. Seven
4. Everyone there was also wasted
5. She's a six-foot blonde who wears spray latex for a living and spends her days either falling over or having sex
6. Looking at Calvin Cutter's designs for 'Trojan' costumes
7. Trampled by a hippopotamus
8. Sex on legs with the IQ of candyfloss
9. Mrs Partridge
10. Max's dropped basket bouncing down the steps
11. Odysseus and Diomedes
12. Someone sounded the Temple and Citadel alarms
13. Professor Penrose
14. Dirk Thrust
15. A holo experience room, to see the Troy holos
16. She was the expert at tidying up after stupid things (and doing stupid things)
17. The eagle attacked him
18. Rosie Lee
19. Leave Astrid in Troy, and pretend she'd left St Mary's to go for a walk, but never came back
20. He was in Sick Bay (with a nasty rash)
21. Because that's when they arrived in Troy the last time
22. Picked up the drone and threw it as far as she could - the eagle went after it

Round Three

Questions

1. Why did the guards let St Mary's go after Astrid had blessed them?
2. What was the agreed-upon traditional St Mary's plan of action?
3. What did Max pose as to get access to Astrid?
4. How did they smuggle Astrid out of the Temple complex?
5. What was Odysseus and Diomedes' mission?
6. What did Max use to get the goats to leave, and incidentally stop the Trojan guards from finding Odysseus and Diomedes?
7. Why would Tempora be very unhappy with Paris?
8. What name did Max come up with on the spur of the moment for an Egyptian Pharaoh?
9. What did Astrid do to Adrian that proved how intelligent she was?
10. What does it mean if you are warm at St Mary's in winter?
11. What unwelcome reminder did Dr Bairstow give Max?
12. What two things did Max think summed up most of human history?
13. Why did Markham provoke Max with a never-ending supply of 'Fun Facts'?
14. What was Markham going to be arrested for?
15. How did Astrid let them know where she was being kept?
16. How did Max deal with the royal priestess who was acting as Astrid's personal attendant
17. What mistake did Diomedes make?
18. Why didn't Max trust Odysseus anyway?
19. What were Max's terrible instructions to Evans?
20. Why did Max think Astrid would take a job at St Mary's?
21. What was Astrid's condition for joining St Mary's?
22. Why did Mrs Partridge want Max to be in Troy that night?

Answers

1. Their dinner was ready
2. Go up to the Temple at dusk, have a poke around, and see what happens
3. A senior priestess of Athena on a mission from Queen Hecuba
4. Disguised her as a soldier
5. To steal the Palladium from the Temple
6. The Sonic Scream
7. He would have shot her new lover Achilles in the heel and killed him
8. Butluvdon-karmese
9. Asked him lots of really good questions about life in Troy
10. Something is on fire nearby
11. That she would have to make the decision when to call it a day in the search for Astrid
12. Stupidity and bad luck
13. Either she would be provoked to doing him a serious injury, or she'd laugh - either would provide her with much needed stress relief
14. Stealing a sacred chicken last time he was in Troy
15. She chanted instructions in English to the crowd
16. Zapped her with a stun gun
17. He turned his back on Odysseus
18. He was the only one of his crew to make it back to Ithaca
19. If the Sonic Scream didn't work, to push her and Markham out of the pod and shoot them
20. To travel, to meet interesting people, to contribute positively to cultural heritage, to be blown up on a regular basis, to be attacked by a homicidal horse, and to be able to pee during the day
21. To be able to travel to Ancient Egypt
22. To make sure Odysseus and Diomedes would escape with the Palladium and ensure that Troy fell

Notes

HISTORY

Reading the St Mary's books is often as educating as it is entertaining.

The sheer quantity of historical information, as well as interesting snippets of trivia, is enough to send many readers scurrying for their favourite encyclopaedia - either paper or digital - to read more about the people, places, and things that the Historians visit through the course of the books.

Here are some questions about those People, Places, Things … And Dodos!

People Round

Questions

1. Which Egyptian god is The Protector of the Dead?
2. What sort of idiot installs his mistress in his wife's house?
3. Who discovered - and opened - Tutankhamun's tomb in 1922?
4. What two names was Herodotus known by?
5. Who was the Archbishop of Canterbury in 1215?
6. Who was the Babylonian King in 565BC
7. Who was Spencer Perceval?
8. How is the artist Alessandro di Mariano Filipepi better known?
9. What was the name of Julius Caesar's wife at the time of his death?
10. What was so special about Pharaoh Hatshepsut?
11. Who was Henry III's regent
12. Who became the lover of Edward II's queen, and overthrew him?
13. Who was George IV's illegal first wife?
14. Which was the only Greek goddess depicted in contemporary art as having golden hair?
15. Who was Edith Swanneschals?
16. Who had some Barons invited to be the King of England after John died?
17. Who was the wife of Charles II?
18. What nickname did Nell Gwyn give herself, to distinguish herself from the King's French Catholic mistress?
19. Who was Butehamun?
20. Who was Piye?

Answers

1. Anubis
2. Julius Caesar
3. Howard Carter and Lord Carnarvon
4. The Father of History or the Father of Lies
5. Stephen Langton
6. Nebuchadnezzar II
7. The only British Prime Minister ever assassinated
8. Sandro Botticelli
9. Calpurnia
10. She was a woman
11. William Marshall
12. Roger Mortimer
13. Maria Fitzherbert
14. Athena
15. Harold's wife
16. Louis VIII of France
17. Catharine of Braganza
18. The Protestant Whore
19. A state sponsored tomb robber, the Opener of the Gates of the Underworld
20. The Kushite king who conquered Egypt

Places Round

Questions

1. Who is the only English king buried at Westminster Abbey?
2. What was the most important animal to the Minoans
3. When Queen Elizabeth wanted to see a play, what happened?
4. Who were the Medjay?
5. What happened to the Roman town of Camulodunum (Colchester) in 60 AD?
6. Which especially designed building had been constructed for the occasion of the Great Exhibition?
7. What event was the Gunpowder Plot supposed to obliterate?
8. What is so special about the dates of 22 February and 22 October in Abu Simbel?
9. What was the Esagila?
10. Where was St George born?
11. How many people died during the great fire of London?
12. What was the Palladium?
13. What was Jebel Barkal?
14. What was Etemenanki?
15. What is the Kushite fold?
16. What were the other two names of Troy?
17. Why were all the rulers of Crete called Minos?
18. What was the Nowruz?
19. What is the precise nature of Ma'at?
20. Which famous archaeologist excavated most of Bronze Age Crete, and called its inhabitants Minoans?

Answers

1. Edward the Confessor
2. Bulls
3. The theatre company went to her at Richmond or Greenwich
4. The Ancient Egyptian tomb police
5. The Britons burnt it to the ground and slaughtered the inhabitants
6. The Crystal Palace
7. The State Opening of Parliament
8. The dawn sunrise shines directly into the temples inner chamber
9. The major Babylonian temple, dedicated to Marduk
10. Cappadocia, Turkey
11. Five
12. The wooden statue of Athena sacred to Troy
13. The sacred mountain of Kush
14. The Tower of Babel
15. A distinctive ridge of flesh on each cheek beside the nose, a feature on all statues and busts of Royalty from the ancient Nubian kingdom of Kush
16. Ilium and Wilusa
17. It was their title, not their name
18. The Persian New Year festival
19. The ancient Egyptian concept of truth, balance, order, harmony, law, morality, and justice
20. Sir Arthur Evans

THINGS ROUND

Questions

1. What did the English Sumptuary Laws restrict?
2. What is a felucca?
3. What did King John lose in The Wash?
4. What was the scary time travel P word?
5. Jam and Jerusalem is the nickname of which institution?
6. What is a jarvey?
7. What did the Cumaean Sibyl offer King Lucius Tarquinus Superbus in return for his country's entire annual budget?
8. What were Henry II and Eleanor of Aquitaine's eight children called
9. Why did Jane Austen never write a scene without a woman present?
10. What is a kuphar?
11. What is a shaduf?
12. What are Shabtis?
13. Why did the English knights throughout the Middle Ages have pudding-bowl haircuts?
14. What is vair?
15. What did one theory suggest Alfred the Great suffered from?
16. What year did Thera erupt?
17. In Ancient Egypt, what was a khat?
18. What is an etui?
19. What is hoggin?
20. What was included in the pay of the skilled builders of the Pyramids at Giza?

Answers

1. What clothing, fabrics, and colours people could wear
2. A small sailing boat remaining virtually unchanged in design since early Ancient Egypt
3. The entire crown jewels, and his household goods
4. Paradox
5. The Women's Institute
6. The driver of a light two-wheeled carriage
7. Nine scrolls
8. The Devil's Brood
9. She didn't know how men spoke to each other without women around
10. A small coracle made of wood and leather
11. A primitive water pump
12. Wooden statues of servants to serve a Pharaoh in the afterlife
13. It provided padding for the helmet without making the forehead or neck sweaty
14. Squirrel fur
15. Crohn's disease
16. 1628BC
17. An overseer's headdress
18. A container for a lady's miniature toilette items
19. A mixture of clay, gravel, and sand, used for pathways and drives
20. Barley and beer

Dodos Round

Questions

1. Where was the living dodo's only known location?
2. Which book first drew public attention to the Dodo, thanks to Teniel's cartoon of it?
3. Which bird is the closest known surviving relative of the Dodo?
4. How many stuffed dodos remain in the world?
5. When was the last widely accepted dodo sighting?
6. What does the word 'dodo' probably refer to?
7. What is the current opinion for the number of eggs a dodo laid in a clutch?
8. How many complete dodo skeletons have been discovered?
9. Which British Isles Zoo uses the dodo as its unofficial mascot?
10. What phrase was first published in the Bangor Daily Whig And Courier, May 1891

The Dodo used to walk around,
And take the sun and air.
The sun yet warms his native ground -
The Dodo is not there!

The voice which used to squawk and squeak
Is now for ever dumb -
Yet may you see his bones and beak
All in the Mu-se-um

(Hilaire Belloc, 1896)

Answers

1. Mauritius
2. Alice's Adventures in Wonderland
3. The Nicobar Pigeon
4. None
5. 1662
6. Dodar - the Dutch word for the knot of feathers on their rump
7. One
8. Two
9. Jersey Zoo (The Durrell Wildlife Park)
10. As dead as a dodo

Notes

REFERENCES

Jodi uses a phenomenal number of sly jokes, clever shout-outs, and arcane references, and frequently shows off her obscure knowledge and the hard work that goes into researching her books.

Where might you have seen these phrases in other works?

Round One

Questions

1. I felt a disturbance in the force
2. I'll be back
3. The roof could have been supported by four elephants standing on the back of a giant turtle
4. Miss Brooke and Mr Bond
5. In space, no one can hear you scream
6. One does not simply walk into Mordor
7. Frodo Baggins
8. Asterix the Gaul
9. My name is Inigo Montoya, prepare to die
10. A till that would spring shut and take your fingers if you weren't careful
11. Nazgûl
12. Feeding gremlins after midnight
13. Meddling with the affairs of wizards is dangerous for they are subtle and quick to anger
14. They think it's all over ... it is now

Answers

1. A line spoken by Obi-Wan Kenobi in Star Wars
2. A promise uttered throughout history and film, probably most famously by Arnold Schwarzenegger in The Terminator
3. The most famous use of this trope is, of course, Terry Pratchett's Discworld, but occurs in Hinduism, Chinese mythology, and the mythologies of some of the peoples of Africa
   Anywhere, in fact, that had turtles and elephants, seems to have produced this myth
   The earliest surviving depiction is an 1877 engraving
4. Brooke Bond was a British tea importing company, famous mostly for it's PG Tips brand
   They were the first British tea company to include Tea Cards in their packs for children to collect
5. The tagline for the film Alien
6. A line spoken by Boromir in The Lord of the Rings
7. The main protagonist of The Lord of the Rings
8. Asterix the Gaul is a long running of pun-laden comic books by (originally) Goscinny and Uderzo
9. A line from the book and film The Princess Bride
10. In Open All Hours, a TV series by Roy Clarke, starring Ronnie Barker and a very young David Jason, the shop contains this exact till
    It has now become a staple trope in many TV comedies
11. The nine Black Riders from Lord of the Rings
12. Feeding Mogwai after midnight turns them into Gremlins, in the film of the same name
13. A warning to would-be meddlers in Lord of the Rings
14. Famous line at the end of the 1966 World Cup by broadcaster Kenneth Wolstenholme as Geoff Hurst scored England's fourth goal

Round Two

Questions

1. They're heeeeeeeeeere
2. This was not the little boy I was looking for
3. Misses Peak & Frean and Mrs Huntley-Palmer
4. You'll never take our freedom
5. "You shall not pass"
6. A Roman Holiday
7. I think I shall miss you most of all, Scarecrow
8. Lay on Macduff
9. Begin at the beginning, go to the end, then stop
10. Believe six impossible things before breakfast
11. He had a mother? Like Grendel
12. Showtime!
13. There was little heavy lifting, and it was out of the wind and rain
14. Kills 99% of all known germs. Dead

Answers

1. A much-quoted line and tagline from the film Poltergeist
2. A reference to the Star Wars line "These are not the droids you are looking for"
3. Peak Freans and Huntley & Palmer are two former British biscuit manufacturers Both brands are owned by Nabisco
4. "They'll never take our freedom" was a line from the 1995 film Braveheart
5. Another Lord of the Rings quote, from Gandalf this time
6. Roman Holiday is a 1953 American romantic comedy, starring Audrey Hepburn as a princess out to see Rome on her own and Gregory Peck as a reporter
7. A line from The Wizard of Oz
   Scarecrow, of course, was the character from the film seeking a brain
8. A direct, and correct, quote from Shakespeare's Macbeth
   Most people misquote it as "Lead on, Macduff"
9. The King's advice to Alice, in Lewis Carroll's Alice in Wonderland
10. The Queen, in Lewis Carroll's Alice Through the Looking Glass, did this sometimes, and it's referred to in Douglas Adams Restaurant at the End of the Universe
11. Grendel's Mother was the second of the fearsome antagonists that Beowulf had to face in the epic poem
12. Used in a similar context by Jack Nicholson as the The Joker in the 1989 film Batman
13. A recurring phrase in Terry Pratchett's Discworld novels, and also the Science of Discworld, "It's an indoor job, with no heavy lifting" refers to a quote from Jack Cohen and Ian Stewart's book "The Privileged Ape"
14. Domestos adverts used almost this exact phrase as their slogan

Round Three

Questions

1. Monstrous regiment
2. "We're doomed!" in a Scottish accent
3. A prophet is never appreciated in his own country
4. Below the salt
5. Keep your friends close and your enemies closer still
6. Afternoon delight
7. And then there were five
8. Inevitable treachery
9. Mr Markham is ready for his close up, Mr De Mille
10. It's alive!
11. Stinking Henry cheese
12. It is better to remain silent and be thought a fool, than to open your mouth and remove all doubt
13. It was a dark and stormy night …
14. Mavis Enderby

Answers

1. The First Blast of the Trumpet Against the Monstruous Regiment of Women is a polemical work by the Scottish reformer John Knox, against the two female monarchs ruling the British Isles in his time, Elizabeth I and Mary Queen of Scots
   It is also the title of a Terry Pratchett book which drew its name from the same polemic
2. Fraser, the Scottish undertaker in the Dad's Army TV series was particularly fond of uttering this prophecy
3. In Luke 4:24 of the King James Bible, the line is "Verily I say unto you, No prophet is accepted in his own country"
4. Below the salt is an idiom referring to someone of lower social standing or importance
   It originates from historical dining practices where salt (an expensive commodity) was only served on the Nobles' top table, and not to the lower orders
5. Despite often being attributed to Machiavelli, actually first used in the film The Godfather Part II
6. "Afternoon delight" is a slang term, often with a sexual connotation, referring to a midday sexual encounter
   It gained popularity due to the 1976 song "Afternoon Delight" by the Starland Vocal Band
7. A line from the Ten Little Indians poem, and also the Agatha Christie novel And Then There Were None
8. "Curse your sudden but inevitable betrayal" is a the most remembered quote from the TV show Firefly
9. Refers to a line from Sunset Boulevard "I'm ready for my close-up, Mr. De Mille"
10. Probably the most well-known line from the 1931 film, Frankenstein
11. There is a British artisanal cheese, named Stinking Bishop, which was awarded the title of The King of Cheese in 2011
12. A phrase that has been attributed to Abraham Lincoln, Mark Twain, and even the Bible, but the first verified source is in a book titled "Mrs. Goose, Her Book" by Maurice Switzer
13. Such a famous and mostly mocked opening for novels, that there is now a prize, the International Bulwer-Lytton Fiction Contest, for any deliberately badly written novel that starts with that line
    It's a bit unfair on poor Edward Bulwer-Lytton, who wrote many excellent works, and also gave us phrases such as "The pen is mightier than the sword", "The almighty dollar", and "The great unwashed"
14. Mavis Enderby is a small village in Lincolnshire

Round Four

Questions

1. Why didn't you ask Evans?
2. The Argonath
3. This too will pass
4. Chief Rice, Miss Boroughs, Technician's Zelazny and Baxter, First Officer Lewis, Scientists Bradbury, Carpenter, and Verhoeven
5. Gin-soaked women dropping their babies down flights of steps
6. Slough of Despond
7. Once more into the breach dear friends
8. An orchid called Audrey
9. GogMagog
10. Polly Perkins
11. "Reader, I carried him"
12. Bringing you in from the cold
13. Prisoner and Escort

Answers

1. Whey Didn't They Ask Evans? is an Agatha Christie novel that has been televised multiple times
2. In The Lord of the Rings, The Argonath, also known as the Gates of Argonath, was a great monument of Gondor
3. There is a story of a king who called his advisors to him and said "Create for me a ring such that when I am happy, and I look at the ring, I will become sad and when I am sad, I will look upon the ring and be happy."
   They went away and returned with a simple ring, engraved with the phrase "This, too, shall pass"
4. Edgar Rice Burroughs, Roger Zelazny, Stephen Baxter, Ray Bradbury, and CS Lewis are all science fiction writers
   John Carpenter and Paul Verhoeven are science fiction film makers
   All have works with connections to Mars
5. Pretty much describes the famous Hogarth engraving Gin Lane
6. The Slough of Despond is a fictional bog from John Bunyan's allegory, The Pilgrim's Progress
   It represents a state of deep depression, despair, or hopelessness
   It is also the nickname for the Berkshire (and Buckinghamshire - it's confusing) town, much ridiculed in Britain
7. From Shakespeare's Henry V, the King's speech at Harfleur
8. In the film Little Shop of Horrors Seymour names his strange alien orchid Audrey 2, after the object of his affection Audrey
9. GogMagog refers to a mythical giant in British folklore, often associated with the legendary founder of Britain, Brutus
   Gog and Magog are also the legendary guardians of London
10. Polly Perkins is an actress and singer/songwriter most famous in the 1960s but more recently for her role in Eastenders
    It is also the name of the heroine of a Music Hall song in the mid-late 19th Century
    And Polly Perks was the protagonist in Terry Pratchett's Monstrous Regiment
11. "Reader, I married him" is a line in the last chapter of Charlotte Brontë's Jane Eyre
12. Resonates somewhat with John le Carré's most famous spy novel "The Spy Who Came In From The Cold"
13. The title of the first ever episode of Porridge, written by Dick Clement and Ian La Frenais, starring Ronnie Barker

Round Five

Questions

1. Test-firing frozen chickens
2. Peshgaldaramesh, Marduk-kabit-ah-heshu, and Ninurta-kudurri-usur
3. There's something nasty in the woodshed
4. Wivenhoe
5. Alexander Knox
6. Rosy fingered dawn
7. Vortigern
8. Full speed ahead and damn the torpedoes
9. Just One Damned Thing After Another
10. Sunflowers, brilliant golds and yellows against a blue background
11. Christopher Barker, dwelling in Paules Churchyard at the signe of the Tygers head
12. Markham

Answers

1. There is a story that Rolls Royce used to fire chickens, turkey, even ducks into the intakes of their jet engines to test their ability to withstand bird strikes. When a US aircraft engineering company tried this, it always shredded the engines. Rolls Royce's advice was "Defrost the birds first"
   The only true bit of this story is that in the 1970s, the US Federal Aviation Administration did have a building for firing (unfrozen) bird carcasses at aircraft and aircraft engines
2. All three are kings of Ancient Babylon
3. In Stella Gibbons' Cold Comfort Farm, Aunt Ada Doom famously saw "something nasty in the woodshed!" (or the potting shed, or the bicycle shed), and was waited on hand and foot and could never be contradicted on anything for decades
   It is also the title of a 1942 mystery novel by Anthony Gilbert, among Douglas Bader's possessions when he arrived at Colditz
4. Wivenhoe is a town in the Colchester area, in Essex
5. Alexander Knox was a prolific Canadian actor and writer, appearing in over 100 film and TV productions, with writing credits for many more
6. A line from Homer's Iliad and Odyssey
   It also appears in Virgil's The Aeneid, but he almost certainly stole it from Homer

7. Vortigern was a 5th Century English warlord, mentioned as King of the Britons by the Venerable Bede
His name in Welsh was Guorthigirn…

8. This famous naval order has entered popular English usage as meaning to carry on regardless of the risk
The order was first issued on 5 August 1864 by Admiral Farragut at the Battle of Mobile Bay, Alabama, during the American Civil War

9. A quote by historian Arnold Toynbee
He never used it himself to refer to history, but he did in a review of another book

10. Vincent Van Gogh's most famous Sunflowers paintings, on a yellow-gold background, are a continuation of his earlier Sunflowers works which are on, yes, a blue background

11. One of the oldest printed works in the British Library is "A treatise of the excellencie of a Christian man, and how he may be knowen" which contains the notice "Imprinted at London by Christopher Barker, dwelling in Paules Churchyard at the signe of the Tygers head"
Christopher Barker, Queen Elizabeth I's printer, also produced the first edition of The Bible in English
This has to be one of the most obscure references in all of Jodi's works

12. I've saved my favourite for last
Richard III, His Life and Character is a book by Clements Markham, and is the only major work to mention the character and behaviour of the two Princes in the Tower
The single longest running spoiler in all of Jodi's books

ACKNOWLEDGEMENTS

Many thanks are due to many people while I worked on this book.

Obviously, firstly to Jodi, for creating the wonderful world in which her books are set, and writing such marvellous characters and stories there, and to Hazel for allowing me to write a quiz book in the first place, and for help and advice.

Then to my wife, Julia, who encouraged me, with very little recourse to whips and chains, to complete it.

And to so many others:

Karin was my first proofreader, and provided many wonderful chapter images.

Debs Pick my first copy editor, finding more errors, spelling mistakes, peculiar grammar (and the only reference ever to orca sex I hope to write) than I would have thought possible.

And many thanks to Sharon, the marvellously patient typesetter.

Printed in Dunstable, United Kingdom

74502102R00161